# ALL THAT AWAITS YOU

## A SHORT STORY COLLECTION

Greer Sickinger-Maher

 Scan the QR code for the read-aloud option. The story is being read by the author herself. If you're traveling or just want to take advantage of this option, please oblige.

# Table of Contents

# The Nun, the Priest, and the Circle Clan

*The child who is not embraced by his village will burn it down to feel its warmth.*

-African Proverb

## December 2010

The snow blew through the air making the old church campus resemble a Medieval Abbey. Its high, majestic brick buildings, complete with high gables and windows. Multiple panels and arches squared off to hug the courtyard. The more she looked, the more she saw. It was built around what would be a garden in a warmer season and it could have been hundreds of years ago or now, if you ignored the McDonald's a few yards away and the gas station a few yards the other way.

The large black metal fence, the would-be garden, and the view of the surrounding brick buildings offered her sanctity and safety. The snow blew harder through the courtyard, whistling. Was there a light on inside?

## Surrounded
## December 24th, 2010
## Affluent Neighborhood in Philadelphia

*She was surrounded.*

*Her heart raced. This was a certain emotional death… the death of something psychological. There was no mental way out, and it didn't let up. She sat in a chair while the others formed a circle, forcing her slowingly outside the group. Yet, she was emotionally surrounded. It was a mental ambush.*

1

*Some moments in life are never forgotten.*

## East Side of Philadelphia
## Christmas Eve 2010

The Salem witch trials were on one of the channels that presents historical documentaries. Actual artifacts and places were shown, and then the show would cut to actor recreations where they would show girls who looked 12-19 years of age sitting in a 17th-century courtroom. They would all start shivering in synchronicity, and then one would look out and pretend to see the accused flying across the courtroom. Then one would pretend to be going into convulsions and as fast as she started, the others followed suit. How did they all know what to do in synchronicity? The commentator suggested they took quick nonverbal cues from one another. It was emotional contagion driven by an increased feeling of importance.

It was time to turn the TV off and begin getting dressed. Briar checked the invitation again. Was she really invited? It was an email addressed to over forty people. It simply said it was time for the "Wild Wolff family celebration" and people should respond with what they wanted to bring. There was an address showing where it would be. It would be at Ledia's home on the west side in a very hilly area. Briar had replied that she would bring butter cookies. This time, her young son would not be with her because it was not her year to have him for Christmas. No one seemed concerned that she would spend Christmas Day alone.

## West Side of Philadelphia
## Christmas Eve

All the Purdue graduates of Briar's age could be found in the larger living room that seemed darker than usual on this winter day. Briar and all of them had been at the university at the same time and had regular stories to remember and share. In fact, Luke and Betsy had met there and married after graduating. Devin and Carry had also been there at the same time. They dated during their senior year and got married years later. Tiffany and Ken had also met at Purdue and married a few years after graduation. Briar entered the dark living room, lit only by the energetic comments of Ken's loud voice teasing Luke. "Luka-Man, it was you who brought a kitten to the Moonshine parade dance as your date. She was the cutest one there at the time! Yeah, he did it to get babes. Present company is the prize!" Ken winked at Betsy.

"I had a kitten named Dude, and it had a little dude rag on its head. My date!" Betsy added, pointing to herself.

"Yup, that's how they met. Each brought a feline as a date. They had to find each other!" The Purdue grads continued laughing and talking over each other, weaving Purdue history, their history, with current Purdue topics. Briar felt grateful for her stepfamily, whom she'd known since she was fourteen, and the coincidence that many of them had chosen Purdue, an added connection. They continued making fun of Dr. Cidel, the famous statistics professor.

Those unlucky enough to have him, would never forget him. Ken stood up and made a stern face like Dr. Cidel, then turned his back on everyone just as the professor used to do when he was thinking. Everyone clapped because they knew what Dr. Cidel was famous for. He quickly shot around and then pounded his fist, saying something in a stuffy voice about

Simpson's Paradox and pretending to draw a diagram in the air, keeping the snotty professor face. People continued to laugh, remembering Dr. Cidel as the unrelatable professor who couldn't be reasoned with. There continued to be talks about philosophy professors and crazy campus events.

"Who actually had Cidel?" Ken asked. Briar and Luke raised their hands reluctantly. A conversation started about the luckier half, who had Dr. Wynette, who was personable and made statistics fun.

Briar wanted to get Luke alone to discuss the Miranda Rights she'd been read a week earlier by two police officers, and how frightened she was. Luke was shorter than Briar at only 5'2", but he always made her feel safe. He spoke with humor and clearly knew his field, having practiced law for fifteen years just outside of DC. Would she be taken as weird? Would she alienate all her Purdue grad stepfamily? Would she then be more lonesome? She decided to stay quiet for a moment. She could hear the loud teasing of the young men still resounding.

"Luke, hopefully you recognize your natural superiority in mixology?" Ken asked as Luke handed him a drink. After the noise died down and people got sandwiches from the potluck table, and Luke handed off drinks that he mixed himself, Briar approached Luke.

"I had a scary experience. I don't know if I need an attorney or not." Suddenly, Luke's face grew serious and mature. He looked right at her.

"What's going on? What happened?" The way he asked made her feel extremely warm and safe. In those simple words came across so much of his wisdom. Briar didn't want to bring negativity to everyone's Christmas Eve revels. She forced herself to laugh slightly as if it wasn't at all that bad.

"I had a really irregular experience. I have consulted with an attorney. I don't think anything will come of the bad experience, but my council stands by." Briar put her finger in the air and tried to laugh at the end of the sentence, to lighten the seriousness of the situation up. Luke stared intensely at her without smiling, the way he would look at a client in a dire situation. His mature law hat drove this look. Briar appreciated his seriousness and the fact that he could see through her. Something had happened, and he knew it.

"What's going on? You can talk to me!" Briar stared out for a moment and just couldn't. She respected Luke and didn't want to give a long-lasting, alienating impression. He finally broke the silence and said, "If you have spoken to council and they have spoken to whoever created the 'irregular experience' you're speaking of ... follow what they say. Don't deviate... okay? You can call me anytime." Briar's face turned red, and she tried to laugh. She could not and would not share that she had been read Miranda Rights.

When she left the police station the day it happened and called an attorney, he had charged her $500 to call the police and ask what was going on. He called her back and spoke so quickly that she almost missed what he said as his words ran together.

"They're-done-with-you. It's-over."

"Are you sure? They aren't lying? I didn't do anything." He quickly interrupted, again speaking entirely too fast. "This-is-iron-clad. Police-are-lazy-and-stupid! It's-over!

Go-enjoy-your-break!" That was the end of the call that took place two days before. Briar still couldn't believe it and continued to feel unsafe. She had filed a perfectly legitimate police report, yet the police had turned it on her as if she had filed falsely. She had then been read Miranda Rights. Even though her attorney said it was "over", he still held a retainer on her insistence, in case the police lied.

Kay could be seen and heard slapping her overweight teenage daughter, Tarrin, in the kitchen. Tarrin could be heard saying something back to Kay, to which Kay yelled back at her. People dispersed from the kitchen to go about their business and give them space, since this was a regular thing with Kay and Tarrin. People made paper plates of food fortheir younger children, watched whatever holiday nonsense was on TV, and asked each other how life was.

Briar still felt disoriented and meandered down to the basement. The basement had kids pedaling on small plastic cars. Down here, Briar found her adopted sister, Nicole, who was the biological relation of everyone under the Christmas Eve roof. Briar and those who married into the family, such as the spouses of her Purdue cronies, were the only

non-biologicals. Briar wanted more than anything a sister. When she had moved back to Philadelphia from California after her divorce, she had found a card that read, "To my sister… just because…" and the inside had a heartfelt message. She had turned it around in her hands and daydreamed that one day she and her adopted sister would be close, and she would mail it to her sister, and they would smile over it. Briar would be needed in her life, she hoped one day. She kept the card safe in a box in her bedroom, sure she could get to the point of mailing it one day. They approached each other to talk about their father, Briar's biological dad, Nicole's non-biological. He was not present at the Christmas Eve gathering due to having a newfound California lifestyle with his new wife, after Nicole's mother passed away.

"What did you think about dad's Christmas card? The whole… we are enjoying California and won't be coming to the east coast for the Wild Wolff Christmas… yada yada yada…?" Briar hoped for a close sister moment. She had hoped for this for a long time and looked for any drop of hope.

"Yeah, that was truly offensive. It was like they don't care about the rest of the world."

"I know… right?!" Briar was satisfied with the conversation so far. They were agreeing and vibing, even if she was initiating negative remarks about her dad.

"I wasn't even that surprised, personally!" Briar went on to share more.

Maybe she would have a real sister. Briar had never wanted to give up on it. Years earlier, when Briar was married and living in San Diego as a stay-at-home mother, she had tried to warn Nicole about their father's new wife. But instead of being in solidarity with Briar, she called their father to say that Briar is "on a rampage" to hurt his third wife. This had caused Nicole to behave in a self-righteous way when their father called Briar to admonish her not to speak ill of his new wife. Shortly after that, their father's new wife had verbally attacked Nicole, saying she was the bastard child of her late mother. Their father didn't come to Nicole's defense. Even then, she didn't call Briar to say, "Wow, you were right!"

Briar had really wanted them to back each other up and stand in solidarity the way she had seen sisters do. Her dad had paid for Nicole's Purdue education just like he paid for hers. Briar felt the least Nicole could do was respect his real daughter.

But now that their father was showing his narcissistic true colors, and as much as Nicole wanted to sound as if she was in *good* with Briar's father, it became a strain. Briar's father was known for his verbal attacks on people, directly or through whoever he was married to, and the uniqueness lay in his low, deep, quiet voice. He could say to her cousin John, who wanted to go kayaking with him, "Why don't you go sail into Alaska and get lost?" or to her other cousin Bill, who had put on weight, "You would have a better job if you looked the way you looked when you were nineteen." These remarks caused people to pause in the moment and later walk away angry.

"Well, he sent me a nice Christmas check that let me be generous to others," Nicole pushed. Briar smiled at her in a way that you smile at a lying ten-year-old. Nicole crossed her arms and went on. "He said he's planning to take me on a trip to Europe. But I'm not sure when."

"Well, look, I'm happy that you think my dad is sending you money and that you want to believe you have a trip to Europe vaguely planned with him. He would verbally go after you the way he verbally goes after everybody except that you seem to have a lot more protection than most of us." Briar signaled with her eyes to the upstairs where all of Briar's stepfamily could be heard stomping around, mixing drinks, eating the potluck mayonnaise dishes, and remarking over the children. This caused Nicole to turn red and stare hard at Briar, as if she needed a rebuttal.

"What matters to me is my husband and my family upstairs. Nothing else! You and I have a long way to go!" This left Briar confused. So if her father was sending Nicole money, why didn't he matter to her? Wasn't she grateful?

Briar couldn't remember if she had asked Nicole that out loud or not. She only received the understanding that she didn't matter to Nicole and never would.

"Let me know when this European trip actually happens.

My dad is *just my dad*. He always felt close to me, whether we appear to be getting along or not. He was perfectly fine with just my brother and me. Your mom insisted he adopt you. I'm glad you have so much protection from his verbal attacks." Briar never knew if she said this aloud or not, but it was the truth and was exactly what she was thinking at the time.

After this, the upstairs atmosphere changed dramatically. Even the lighting changed inside while the snow blew harder outside. Word traveled abnormally quickly in this stepfamily and now their conversation, which Briar didn't believe she said anything wrong, was related to the whole stepfamily, except maybe the Purdue graduates who were too busy comparing the *Black Eyed Peas* and *Lady Gaga* to the *Cure* and *U2* playing in the late 1980's and the coffee campaign to get the whole campus addicted to coffee when they were in college.

Briar felt the haunt everywhere else. She thought maybe Kay would help her now that she was done slapping her daughter. Nicole's mother had died of cancer ten years earlier and would have wanted the girls to be close, especially Briar's young son and Nicole. Maybe Briar could speak to Kay, who was Nicole's aunt? Maybe Kay would advocate for Briar to be treated as a sister and with respect.

"Hey, so I don't matter to Nicole? I'm her sister..."
"Nicole is my niece... and you? Well, I'm glad you like coming to our parties!" Kay then turned around. Word traveled fast to Kay. Briar was confused and pulled a chair up where Kay and all her sisters, Nicole's aunts, sat and talked.

They formed a circle that got tighter and tighter. Lydia, Kay, Reba, May, and all of them made a circle that focused on Nicole. Tall, tattooed, body-pierced Nicole, their niece, who just finished her cigarette on the porch. Somehow, Briar's chair was slowly pushed out of the circle. As they subtly tightened the circle, Briar had to keep moving her chair back a little at a time until she was outside of the circle. Briar felt her heart race and the blood rush to her face. She was outside the circle as they moved their chairs in and began a verbal love bomb of comments to reassure Nicole. They talked about her great-grandmother, her heritage, and her many relatives, and made Nicole the absolute focus. They all made extreme eye contact with Nicole. They continued the conversation that included *only Nicole* and their family heritage, and how it all connects to Nicole. Briar felt more than awkward; she felt *pain*.

She daydreamed that the room would get dark and the only light would be her father busting through the door and screaming, *"Don't you ever treat my daughter Briar like this! She is just as important as Nicole. She's already spending Christmas alone and you bitches pull this shit? A circle around Nicole, push your chairs so she has to move hers back, and experience being more and more outside the circle? Come on Briar, we're going!"* During the daydream, she pictured the front door open and the snow blowing in.

But Briar knew she couldn't dream a rescue mission into existence. The pain was psychologically excruciating. Her next daydream was that someone would move their chair back and start a conversation with her. She would smile and they would talk, whoever it was. This daydream made her look for signs. Was someone backing their chair up? Wait… the legs on that chair look like they're moving. She daydreamed that sweet-dimpled Reba, one of the step cousins who was never seen being anything but kind and smiling, would move her chair back and ask her how she's doing. She would show concern for Briar spending Christmas alone the following day and would invite her. She would have genuine love, care, and concern for her. They would bond, and the relationship would continue beyond Christmas. *But this was Briar's imagination.* Reba never moved her chair.

Eventually, Briar got up and left, and got into her car, and tripped on the yard sign that read *Merry Christmas* and *Welcome,* cutting her ankle slightly. She drove home. No one who saw her leave said goodbye. When she left, she heard her Purdue cronies talking about meditation and how it can give wisdom you never thought you had. She saw out the corner of her eyes, Ken imitating a person in a yoga-style meditation, and the girls defending meditation. They would gladly wish Briar well, but she knew that her strife would show on her face. She felt the burn of her tears as she drove, complete with Christmas Carols on the radio.

The next day, she had called the church to make an appointment with the priest and nun to discuss her feelings and better understand what had just happened. When Briar arrived at the family gathering, she had already been in a state over the police incident and not having her son for Christmas. She now felt substantially worse. When she had left the house earlier, after watching the Salem Witch Trial documentary, she was already glum. Now she wished she had stayed home.

The snow blew through the air, making the old church campus resemble a Medieval Abbey with its high, majestic brick buildings with high gables and windows with multiple panels, and arches squared off to hug the courtyard. The more she looked, the more she saw. It was built around what would be a garden in a warmer season. It could have been hundreds of years ago or now if you ignored the McDonald's a few yards away and the gas station a few yards the other way.

The large black metal fence, the would-be garden, and the view of the surrounding brick buildings were sanctity and safety for the eyes. The snow blew harder through the courtyard and could be heard whistling. Was there a light on inside?

She would walk right through this courtyard, as the fence was open, just for her. She waited in the church and prayed. Her thoughts raced the way they do when recovering from a trauma.

She had called an hour before to make the appointment when a middle-aged sounding lady answered and booked her. She had, however, explained that she was almost off for the day and let her know that she would be leaving the church soon, and the phone would then ring to voicemail. She was asked if she had the correct church. She had answered that yes, like most places, there's a McDonald's and a gas station nearby, so this is the correct church.

The priest, Father Francis, and the nun, Sister Mary Margaret, smiled widely and led Briar into a cozy room with a fireplace. She sat in a comfortable chair that looked like Elder Brewster's chair from days of old. They seemed to have nothing to do that day but welcome Briar on Christmas. Briar felt at this moment that *she mattered*. They made time for her, and they smiled warmly at her. She was not *in trouble* with being read Miranda Rights, she was not *in trouble* for wanting to be respected by someone who is supposed to be her sister, who so freely takes money from her father without respecting anyone in Briar's biological family. In this moment, she felt just right.

"So, what seems to be troubling you? How can we listen?" Father Francis started.

"Yes, that's what we're here for!" Sister Mary Margaret added. Briar felt relieved in a way she had not felt in a long time. *She felt safe.*

"I do appreciate your seeing me on Christmas Day. I know it's a busy day and a lot is going on." Briar realized how quiet everything was today. There was nothing, no noise, no cars outside, no people, just serenity.

"This is what we do! We are in the business of understanding and healing." Sister Mary Margaret added. She seemed to be knitting something while listening. This made Briar feel even more heard. Her knitting meant she was planted down and ready. Father Francis had a calm smile.

"What happened?" But Briar felt like Father Francis already knew.

"I was surrounded. They made a circle at a family gathering, and I was outside the circle. They seemed to all read each other's minds and be in synchronicity. They just moved and talked together as if it was rehearsed but it wasn't." Briar's eyes rapidly moved as she spoke.

"That doesn't sound like much of a loving family." Father Francis smiled calmly. Briar felt loyalty to her situation.

Loyalty was something she hadn't felt in a long time. "They are actually a stepfamily," Briar explained. "That explains a lot. Do they love you?"

"No, I believe they tolerate me. They love each other." Briar continued explaining and couldn't believe how quickly she had identified that truth in her life.

"Why then were you there?" Father asked again with a slight smile.

"I want a family, that's all. I'm lonely."

"Do you think a stepfamily can love you as much as their own? There are really strong step families but the majority struggle." Father looked surprised by the very idea that they could consider loving Briar as much as their own. It seemed to Briar that Father Francis and Sister Mary Margaret already knew everything. They seemed very naturally aware of what had happened.

"Well, I have an adopted sister, and my father loves me more than her for sure." Briar shook her head gently as she said that.

"I'll bet they all know that, including the adopted sister.

Do you think the circle had something to do with their disliking her reality?" Father Francis smiled as he spoke. This made Briar feel supported. It was as though he knew her whole situation, and it was written in his heart. Sister Mary Margaret also smiled slightly.

"My dad always said he could never love an adopted kid

more than my brother and me. We got along fine until he got around the stepfamily. Then, it was like he wanted to prove to them the opposite, so he pretended to dislike me in front of them. But somewhere inside, do they actually believe my own dad dislikes me?" Briar posed her fact as a question.

"If they love their own more than anyone unrelated, then they would also project that onto your father, and somewhere deep inside, they would be bothered by knowing that he would also love a biological family more." Father looked so calm.

"How did they make that circle so quickly and begin playing off each other's words without any rehearsal?" Briar asked the room, not expecting an answer.

"Neurodivergent individuals are susceptible to emotional contagion." Father Francis said this, then he and Sister Mary Margaret looked at each other and laughed as Briar's response was what they would expect, a tilted head look of slight confusion. Father Francis went on to explain. He had purposely said it quickly, the way Mary Poppins says, "supercalifragilisticexpialidocious."

"In clan-like, small-town families, it's not uncommon for there to be a tendency to absorb, catch, or influence or be influenced by each other's feelings in the moment. Also, the whole German Catholic thing." Father Francis and Sister Mary Margaret both laughed out loud at the last part. Briar still looked a little confused, but was starting to understand, just a little.

"Passive aggression is rampant in German Catholics.

When you combine that with the whole small-town thing, neurodivergence and emotional contagion… oh we have the perfect storm! You were excluded from the circle but actually psychologically surrounded, bullied." Father Francis still smiled a bit, making Briar feel that she was okay, that it was somebody else's problem. Briar nodded but had to ask what he meant about emotional contagion. Sister Mary Margaret spoke this time, with a slight smile and still knitting, the fire crackling in the background, and the snowy wind blowing visibly outside. This could have been now or two hundred years ago.

"When one person's emotions and behavior directly trigger similar emotions and behavior in others, this is a phenomenon. Did you ever study the Salem…" As Sister started to say it, she and Briar spoke at the same time.

"*Salem witch trials*!" Briar shared with them that she had been watching a documentary on it right before leaving for the Christmas party. She had seen how the girls engaged in emotional contagion by acting in synchronicity. They all noted the small village of the 1600s versus the closeness of the current stepfamily on the west side of town and how they were similar, regardless of the difference in the timeline. Briar felt she could breathe better. She had only wanted to have a sister and a family and to feel loved. Somehow, the insecurity people had in the knowledge of the reality that Briar would always be her father's favorite and only daughter, caused them to overprotect Nicole. This was not due to the loss of her mother, Briar explained. It had gone on prior to this.

"Studies prove that our brains feel the same pain when we are excluded socially as when we have physical pain. The dorsal anterior cingulate cortex and the anterior insula show the same activity during social exclusion and physical pain." Sister continued knitting as she spoke. Briar smiled as she knew these were her people. It was like they knew her for her whole life and had watched everything. They were firmly loyal to her in a way she had needed someone to be for a long time.

They continued their questions that led Briar to confirm what she knew to be true. They asked who moved their chair to let her in and if anyone looked concerned about the aggressive way she was pushed out of the circle. Briar shrugged her shoulders, and looked helpless, and shook her head no.

"Look, I said some mean truths. I felt they needed to be said. Maybe that set off the way they psychologically surrounded me by way of exclusion." Briar believed that she had pounded down her reality to Nicole in a way she wasn't ready to accept.

"Well, did you lie?" Father seemed almost amused. "No, I definitely didn't lie."

"The truth is a painful thing to accept. Do you know what else is a painful weapon… more powerful than pepper spray? Intentional exclusion." Father Francis looked smart, confident, and non-accusatory.

"So when I was read Miranda Rights, I knew I was alone in the world. No one would help me, and this just confirmed it. All I've ever wanted was to be any woman, just any woman with a family." Briar shook her head with tears now running down her face. She closed her eyes for a while and turned her head to the ceiling, breathing carefully. This moment was golden and holy and designed to give Briar what no one else would give her… loyalty.

"It sounds terrifying! But I'll bet you're strong and will prevail. There's no reason you won't. I suspect you're not any woman, you're not *anybody*. I suspect you have some outlying qualities. When we were on a mission in Africa, we gained so much wisdom. One African proverb states that *the child who is not embraced by his village will burn it down to feel its warmth*. It's not limited to a child. They were burning your village while you were protecting it. If Nicole's truth didn't fit into their village, they would burn it."

Briar never wanted to leave their safe Christmas haven.

She barely remembered going there or leaving, but she remembered well what it looked like. Mostly, she reveled in the kindness and healing that was shown to her.

When she called them a week later to express gratitude, there seemed to be no such phone number. She called the Archdioceses. No one seemed to have the phone number or knew anything about Father Francis or Sister Mary Margaret. No one had heard of them. Finally, Briar got in the car to drive back to their church. There was the McDonald's, the gas station, and a dirt lot with some fallen stones from a former building. The fallen stones were the size and style she remembered the church being. Was this a church two hundred years ago? Briar walked around the dirt lot, almost in circles. She could see the snow and mud under her feet. She felt the bandage attached to her ankle from when she left the Christmas party and was stabbed by the sign that read, *"Merry Christmas & Welcome"*. She was bundled up for the snow and breathing hard while considering the Dr. Cidel type of statistical likelihood that she had a supernatural experience or a deep meditation. She had the wisdom to stop wishing for a sister and the knowledge that *anyone* was capable of using words and actions to burn down a village to feel its warmth. Briar knew she was more than *anyone*.

# St. Francis Academy
## Unfug an einem Wintertag
## Mischief on a Winter Day

## Saint Francis Academy for Girls
## Cincinnati, Ohio 1984

Saint Francis sits in the same place as the day it was founded in 1873. The chapel hall was still lined with marble statues and had Italian tile flooring. Many of the older parts of the building remain unchanged since its opening, complete with marble fireplaces. The sisters of the convent still lived upstairs. But there's a painting there that was hung at the end of the 1984 school year because it won an award. It was painted by a senior. To this day, only four students know the backstory of the painting, and it will not be revealed. Those who know find it cryptic as it sits there, almost laughing at any beholder who doesn't know the story and the way it makes a fool of anyone stopping to view.

That day in 1984, the snow on the roads was cleared but remained piled to the sides. East Walnut Hills had a regular flow of cars traveling by. Girls filed into the church hall and scattered into the various hallways where they found their lockers. Today, it looked the way it always looked. Girls were rolling their leggings off, or folding them under their skirts, putting their cigarettes in their bras, sneaking make-up on, and ensuring it looked "natural" as they sometimes had to wipe parts of it off. Sister Francesca walked by and, without stopping, used her right hand to quickly rip a picture of Rob Lowe off the inside of a girl's locker. Sister continued walking without turning around as the girl yelled after her, "He's my cousin, honestly! It's a family picture." Her voice faded at the last part of her sentence since she knew she wouldn't get the picture back. The other girls looked sympathetic at Mina since some knew that Rob Lowe may actually be her cousin from Cincinnati.

"Today's the day!" Sybil whispered to her freshman sister, Ramey, before she made her way to the senior hallway. Shay, Sybil's best friend in the senior class, shook her head at Sybil.

"We're flying too close to the sun," she warned Sybil in a whisper. Sybil walked confidently down the hall with her long blond hair waving from the bottom, where it almost touched the middle of her back. She had some loose curls that she didn't have to work very hard to create. Sybil's height that lorded above most of the seniors, combined with her face that most found worthy of the Ford Modeling Agency, meant some girls stepped out of her way. Shay was equally pretty but with opposite coloring. Shay had long, dark hair and big brown eyes, dimples, and stood slightly shorter next to Sybil. Shay found that Sybil triggered nervousness in her when she did unexpected things. At last spring's May Crowning, when they were juniors, Sybil casually lit a cigarette and kept it down by her side, puffing on it while she sang just as devoutly as the rest. But a bee had stung a girl nearby, and everyone ran to avoid it. Sybil was left standing unshaken, puffing on her cigarette, but now visible to all. She looked unfazed when she was brought into Mother Superior's office.

"I need to remind you that we are to honor the Blessed Mother during May Crowning." Sister stared hard at Sybil. Sybil returned her stare with a casual, confused look, sitting calmly as if she owned the school.

"Smoking during the May Crowning is prohibited." Mother Superior doubled down on her directive and nodded firmly.

"I haven't seen that in the handbook. It actually says that the May crowning honors the mother of Jesus via crowning the statue. We leave winter behind and welcome spring. It says nothing about no smoking." Sybil spoke as if she were educating Mother Superior, who now sat with wide eyes, as if she were searching for the right words.

"I believe the handbook is clear that there is no tobacco, alcohol, or drugs permitted on campus." Mother Superior reminded her, in a calm, low voice.

"No, actually it doesn't say that." Sybil's strength was in her lack of emotion at times when others would be anxious.

"Well, if it doesn't say it, then we will add it." Mother Superior said, in an almost agitated voice. The Saint Francis Academy handbook did not, in fact, specify that one could not smoke during the May Crowning because it was understood, she thought, that this would not be done.

"I'm sweating like a pig!" Shay said to Sybil. Shay longed to have the coolheaded confidence that came naturally to Sybil. She had hidden when Sybil was seen with the cigarette at last spring's May Crowning. This blustery winter day was no different. "Well, it's 18 degrees out in the thick of winter, so I'm not sure why," Sybil spoke while looking around, as if she hardly cared whether Shay sweated or not.

"It's because the Thompson Twins are playing. I always sweat when the Thompson Twins are playing!" Shay sounded desperate.

"There's no music. There's no excuse for you." Sybil still spoke as if she didn't care, as they walked down the hall.

"No, if I even so much as hear the Thompson Twins playing in my brain, I sweat!" Shay pointed her left and right forefingers to her head, anxiously.

Sybil handed a note to a freshman named Cora as they walked by. Cora was new to Cincinnati and the Catholic parochial schools. Sybil loved her southern accent and wanted to give Cora a chance to hang out, compliments of her rogue style.

"And so Cesar made the monumental decision to cross the Rubicon, thereby making history! This is why we say someone has crossed their Rubicon. Now for Cesar's rivalry with Pompey Magnus!" Sister Elizabeth spoke excitedly as if she had just invited everyone to eat cake. She had been marching in place while describing the crossing of the Rubicon. Some girls' feet started marching under their seats, while others nodded, impressed with Sister Elizabeth's enthusiasm.

"Have you girls ever known someone pompous?" Sister asked. Everyone nodded a little, looking around, smiling.

"Well, Pompey Magnus is the reason we have that expression. He took credit for what others accomplished."

Romey and Cora listened while checking the note Cora received from Romey's sister, Sybil. It read that they would "go cruising" after they came up with an escape plan. They looked at each other, shrugging their shoulders.

Down in the senior hall, could be heard the echo of Sister Helen Marie asking girls to find dramatic irony, fatal flaws, paradox, oxymorons, and pathetic fallacy in what they had read so far. Sybil already found all of them and was getting the highest grade in this senior Shakespeare class.

The girls in front of them could be heard complaining with nasally midwestern accents.

"My feet are turning purple. Look at this!"

Sybil laughed a little at hearing them.

When Sister split them into small groups and had them spread out into the hallway and partially in the classroom, Sybil knew she had her escape plan. She reached behind her and opened the back window, signaling to Shay, who looked at her reluctantly. They looked cautiously at the girls with the purple feet who turned around.

"Shut it after us!" Sybil made her demand, pointing at them, and they nodded. No one wanted to challenge the beautiful and forward Sybil.

"It's 18 degrees out!" Shay stepped down, looking helpless but excited about their escape and the adventure that was ahead.

"Actually, it's dropped to 11 degrees, but I'll sing the Thompson Twins to warm you up," Sybil said calmly.

"Sweating to the Thompson Twins! See? It sounds like a Richard Simmons aerobics routine." Sybil swayed to her own singing. The timing was ideal as they walked toward the back blacktop that dipped down toward the parking lot. Ramey and Cora sat, surrounded by other freshmen who bit into their sandwiches, talked, and showed magazine pictures of their favorite celebrities. Slowly, Ramey and Cora excused themselves and made their way toward the bathroom, but went out the side door, exactly how Sybil instructed. She knew to avoid setting off the alarm.

"Well, y'all know how to kick up your boots, huh? Where are we going?" Cora asked, laughing and wide-eyed as she looked around at the snow that had been shoveled to the side. They ran down a hill on the side of the building so no one would see. Sybil and Shay pulled their car up, and Ramey and Cora jumped in. It was unclear if Sybil and Shay even knew where they were going. Sybil would sneak out just because she could. As long as Shay had known her, she had been chasing something.

As they drove, Cora spoke excitedly from the back seat.

"Did y'all know I had never seen snow until I moved here?"

"No, I did not!" Sybil answered quickly as if she actually did truly care, viewing Cora through her rearview mirror and smiling slightly, the way mothers do.

"I love the red brick buildings and the way the trees look in summer, so green. Where I come from, we just have a shopping mall, small ranch houses, funnel cakes, Dairy Queen, and the same ole dust blowing all year. There's not much change of seasons and landscape."

Sybil continued smiling a bit when Cora spoke.

"Cincy is German. You don't know that?" Sybil spoke quickly but still sounded friendly.

"I believe my last name is German too."

"It is for sure!" Sybil answered. She had a knack for knowing the origin of last names without any research. She could even tell the difference between last names in the Far East. No one knew where she got this ability, not even Sybil.

"Wagner is German?" Ramey asked.

"Most certainly!" Sybil calmly drove as if life were easy. Shay looked from her passenger side and smiled at the man in the next car. He drove an ocean blue Rolls-Royce. Shay continued to eye him. Sybil smiled slightly. He signaled Shay to roll her window down, which she did. They couldn't hear each other over the cold wind and traffic. Finally, he caught up with them at a quieter traffic light. Shay began speaking in an accent like Cora's. Ramey and Cora grinned at each other. Sybil sat smoking and was unfazed.

"Well, glory be! We are here for a concert."

"Say we're going to the Police concert at Riverfront!" Ramey added in a whisper, as if this would make her quest to see The Police performing more real.

"No, Neil Diamond. He can't find out we're in high school." Sybil again had all the answers and spoke them just as calmly as always, as she smoked.

"Yes, Neil Diamond! That's right!" Shay really had a good southern drawl going, and the man smiled at her, amused. She maintained an older persona about her. Cora sat nodding, impressed. Shay looked at everyone in the car questioningly.

"Say yes! Say you'll meet him at Riverfront tonight." Sybil instructed Shay in response to the man's request that they go together to the concert, meeting there since they don't know each other. Shay was uncommonly pretty, similar to Sybil, and this happened to her often.

"Well, now how old do y'all think he is?" Cora asked, impressed with the car and the age, whatever it was. She seemed to ask this as if the higher age and price of the car ranked all of them as having obtained something worthy.

"Don't give it to him!" Ramey insisted to Shay that she not give out her phone number, simply because her parents would answer the phone and want to know who was calling. Shay continued pretending to live out of state by using a regional accent.

"Here, give him my cousin's number. She lives in the dorm at UC, so she'll take messages for you." Sybil quickly said the number, again speaking with no emotion, as if solutions in life come easily. The man smiled, blew a kiss to Shay, flipped his brows, and had to hit the accelerator since the light changed. Shay had screamed to him something about meeting at Eden Park.

Their stop at the Eden Park included a look at the view, jumping on the snowy piles that had been plowed, and eating the ice cream they had stopped to get at Graeters. Sybil wanted to ensure that Cora had tried the famous Cincinnati ice cream from Graeters. Ramey and Cora were attempting to ice skate on the frozen pond while Sybil and Shay sat on the bench. Sybil sat expressionless and unshaken as always. Shay danced her upper body, giddy and hoping the man in the Rolls-Royce would drive up.

The ocean blue Rolls-Royce drove up and parked slowly, as if a royal celebrity had pulled up. Sybil looked unfazed. Shay jumped and said in a loud whisper, "He's here! We got so lucky!"

To her surprise, two young men got out of the car. Shay looked at Sybil in disbelief. Cora and Ramey giggled and then headed off to the icy pond to skate, using the boots they wore. Shay looked at Drake as if she needed an explanation for there being another man in the car.

"I'm his driver, it's not my car. I'm a senior at Xavier U." Drake laughed at his confession. Shay shot him a disappointed stare.

"Okay, then who is *he*?" Shay demanded to know who the older gentleman was. He was taller, looked to be in his thirties, and had very light features, complete with curly blond hair, light eyes, and skin.

"I'm Wolfgang, the nephew of the weasel. Jimmy 'the weasel' Fratianno." He spoke in a German accent.

"You sound proud and pompous," Shay said, almost amused. Sybil sat smoking, unreadable.

"I've got connections everywhere." Wolfgang said, looking off into the view of the city and all the snow.

"Those are Italian sounding-names, and you're Wolfgang and you're speaking in a German accent." Shay had to point out what was obvious to her.

"We were part of the Russo gang from Sicily. Some of us were from Germany." Wolfgang laughed.

"How's the witness protection program working out for the other half of your family?" Shay asked, still amused. Sybil sat, taking it all in. This made Wolfgang more interested in the aloof and beautiful Sybil. He continued looking right at her, and the smile never left his face, as she stared straight ahead at the view. Shay continued sounding anxious. Drake looked younger, and now that they knew it wasn't his car, Shay was less interested. He was just a college kid hired to drive for Wolfgang. Drake tried to talk to Shay, who was trying to interrogate Wolfgang.

"How many banks has your family scammed? How many people have they killed?" Shay asked, without reserve. Wolfgang continued grinning, as if he were above any reproach. Drake still wanted to know Shay, so he attempted to ask her questions, not concerned about her questioning Wolfgang.

"When do you graduate? When are you eighteen so I can ask you out?" Drake asked his questions to Shay like a desperate schoolboy.

He looked at her intently, clearly not ready to give up. Shay stared at Wolfgang with intrigue about who he was. He owned a Rolls-Royce and was related to the Ohio mob from Cleveland? Shay was not frightened at all, but unlike Sybil, she *did* ask questions. Sybil continued to sit smoking and looking out at the view.

Ramey and Cora were skating in the distance. They twirled and pulled each other's arms to drag each other across the ice, giggling the entire time.

Wolfgang continued speaking in his German accent.

"I will get my cousin Enzo Delsanter. You know who he is?" Sybil still sat as though Wolfgang didn't exist. Shay made full eye contact and showed intrigue. Shay's reaction was what Wolfgang desired from Sybil, the mysterious beauty.

"My thought exactly is that you do not. He is Tony Dope's kid. Does that enliven your thoughts?" Wolfgang spoke with a deviant German accent and had a hint of threat. Shay just giggled like the schoolgirl that she is. Sybil behaved as though Shay only spoke to an invisible friend. Drake didn't notice that the girls were not from below the Mason-Dixon line. They no longer used the Southern drawl and were unafraid to admit they attended Saint Francis Girls' School.

"Wir sind überall vorbereitet. Das liegt in der Familie. We come prepared everywhere. It runs in the family." Wolfgang sensed that Sybil understood German, and she did. He pulled his jacket back and showed his firearm under his coat, and then his pocketknife.

"Das ist ein Camillus Pilotenmesser von 1983." Sybil finally spoke calmly in German without looking at anyone, as if it were a quiz on knives. She had noted the type of knife it was and the year it was made. She continued with no emotion to look out at the view. Shay had never understood the lack of emotions in Sybil, combined with her large knowledge base.

"Does it matter? Weapons are weapons!" Shay spoke as if it were urgent, got up, and now wanted protection from Drake, who had been trying to talk to her this whole time. Sybil continued smoking while looking at the Eden Park view. Drake grinned and stood in front of Shay as she attempted to hide behind him. Drake was calm, and since he knew Wolfgang, he didn't behave as if he foresaw any danger. He continued laughing, enjoying protecting pretty Shay.

Ramey and Cora were still skating, stopping only when Shay yelled for them. Shay was unclear whether she should tell the girls to run for help or come close so they could get in the car. The girls stopped in a pose as if they were in a painting. Ramey wore a plaid green and navy jacket with a pink scarf and a black bonnet on her head, and Cora wore a long yellow coat with a navy-blue scarf and a bright red barrette. Both girls posed facing each other, but looking straight at Shay. This snapshot could be now or a hundred years ago. This moment in time would make the ideal painting, thought Sybil, who could draw and paint so well that she had won awards. Sybil put her hands up in a square frame, wishing she could paint them. They needed to leave Eden Park by 1:45 so as not to be discovered cutting school.

"It's 1:45. I'm going with or without you all because I'm not losing my scholarship to Brown." Sybil announced this and stood up, tossing her cigarette. Drake and Wolfgang had already realized that the four girls were local and in high school. The girls skipping school was also noticed and met with amusement. Drake turned Shay around to face him, smiled at her, and said, "We're meeting at the concert tonight, right?" Shay smiled at him, feeling safer. "Let's say the *Police* and Gordon Sumner instead of Neil Diamond." Shay smiled shyly. Drake knew she was not as old as she said earlier. They both smiled.

"And don't worry about Wolfgang. They don't target civilians." Drake laughed as he shared this and noted Shay's reaction. Shay wanted to laugh, but instead reached for her pen, since Drake needed her phone number. She wrote down her number, eyeing Drake in a flirty way, after fumbling for something in her purse to write on. Ramey and Cora continued skating, but were coming toward her intently as if they had seen something.

"She's gone! Sybil left us here!" Cora and Ramey spoke almost in unison. Shay smiled nervously, not wanting it to be true.

"I've also got a scholarship lined up for next year, so what makes her think I can afford to get caught cutting class?" They all turned around and looked toward where Sybil had parked, and sure enough, her car was gone. Wolfgang and Drake grinned at the three girls. "We can drive you to your school. We can drop you off at your playground.' Wolfgang spoke in a demeaning way, since he knew the girls had lied about their ages.

It was now closer to two o'clock. If the girls were late for chapel, they could potentially get demerits and all that goes with it. Shay had the most to lose. The girls looked at each other. Ramey and Cora had no idea that Wolfgang had weapons or who his family was. They walked toward his car excitedly saying, "Hurry up, y'all! We don't want to get grounded!" Ramey was not at all surprised by her sister, Sybil, leaving them at the park.

"Does she do this a lot?" Cora asked.

"Well, she sticks her neck out for no one. Let's just say that." Ramey answered. Shay did the sign of the cross while she got into the front seat, slightly more confident in the fact that Drake was Wolfgang's driver.

As they drove, Wolfgang shared, in his German accent, that Sybil didn't go back to school. He had his uncle take her somewhere. Ramey looked confused at Cora. "Then why is her car gone? That's my big sister by the way!" Ramey looked angry and more mature than usual. Wolfgang continued laughing, cleaning his fingernails with his pocketknife.

Wolfgang seemed quite comfortable with being driven regularly by Drake, and it was evident that he knew nothing else in life other than to be served. Shay just watched the road, completely filled with adrenaline, to ensure they were in fact returning to Saint Francis Academy. Drake continued laughing as he drove. He drove faster than usual. He even ran a light. Shay hoped they would get pulled over. She envisioned her parents talking to the police about the missing girls. She could see, in her mind, the entire school gathered in front with the press. Where would they take them? Would it be an unsolved mystery that would haunt their school for decades? Drake turned the radio on, still grinning. Of all bands, the Thompson Twins were playing. Shay was already sweating, and now it was worse.

Finally, she saw him turn by an old bowling alley near the school.

"Take this!" Wolfgang handed Cora a small bag. She barely had time to know what it was. When Shay opened the front door and got out, the younger girls followed. Drake tried to smile at Shay and signal with his fist to his head that he would call her, but she ran with the others across the street. They snuck into the side door, walking around the construction that took place on the side of the school. Sybil had left it cracked since she was a pro at sneaking out. Shay looked at the girls and knew they had less than a minute to head down the chapel hall into the church. She reminded them to fake menstrual cramps in order to combat potential demerits if they were late. They were within a second of being late as they entered and sat quickly in the back. Everyone stood for the opening. They looked around to see if they could find Sybil in the crowd of 300 girls. The girls exchanged glances to read each other's faces to know if any of them had seen Sybil. Cora and Ramey shook their heads no as they looked at Shay.

At the sign of peace, girls walked around hugging. Cora could be seen hugging a friend in her freshman class. Near her feet, she had dropped the small bag that Wolfgang had given her a few feet from the church piano. The bag was quickly picked up and put inside the piano. Was that Sybil? When the girls were seated again, the music started, and it was obviously Sybil playing the church piano and singing along with the choir. Cora attempted to eye Shay. Ramey, Cora, and Shay exchanged glances, unsure how they were left at Eden Park with the nephew of a Cleveland mobster who carried weapons.

Shay sat in church breathing hard, still feeling the adrenaline from the ride and its uncertainty. She thought about Drake. Who was he? Why was he there? He never seemed to stop smiling. He clearly found her interesting and wanted to know her better. She pictured them at the altar getting married. She would have a beautiful dress with white flowers stitched into the outer part. Drake would be handsome in his tuxedo. Then the daydream changed, and she pictured Wolfgang opening fire on some mobsters who were invited to the wedding. There would be a bloody massacre that would make headlines. Shay shook off the daydream. She had heard about the Cleveland mob and various fraudulent activities.

Sybil continued singing *"Be Not Afraid"* as she played the piano, joined by the choir. The lyrics seemed ironic to Shay, Ramey, and Cora. Shay shook her head with slightly angry laughter as she heard her longtime best friend singing a song rooted deeply in sincere faith and Biblical understanding. Sybil had always been impossible to read. Shay thought of what it means to "cross a Rubicon" and what this might mean in her friendship with Sybil.

The art room was busy that day. The pottery wheel was going, the kiln was visible, the paints were out, and artists were spread around the old circular room which had windows all around. Approaching the room, from another part of the building, one would see the back of Sybil as she painted. Her long blond hair flowed down her back. The windows circle her in the wide room, as the other artists pursue their projects. As Sybil paints, a viewer can see a frozen pond, icicles on the trees, two figures emerging, seemingly facing forward, but their heads are looking at each other. Sybil used navy blue and green for one of the coats, she used pinks and reds for hats and scarves, and painted a bonnet on one of the girls. She used a rich yellow to paint a long coat on one of the skaters. They wore no skates, however, just snow boots. She painted the backs of people viewing the two skaters from benches where they could take in the view. One had long blond hair with each arm resting on the top of the bench, in a confident posture. If you looked carefully, it looked like there was a cigarette between the fingers of the blond subject. Two well-built men stood near the benches. One was painted in a side profile, and a slight grin could be seen on his face. The other man had a back profile with blond curly hair. They were both well-dressed. If you looked carefully at the painting, you could see a small pocketknife used to clean his fingernails. As Sybil painted the winter wind blowing in the painting, she knew that his long winter coat would blow back, exposing a firearm. Finally, she dipped her brush in the dark-brown paint since it was time to paint Shay with her dark-brown eyes and hair. She studied the painting carefully.

Where would Shay go? Would she sit on the bench? Would she be protected by Drake? Would she be confronting Wolfgang? *Shay's place in her life became a mystic question that went beyond the decision related to her place in the painting.* When she did finally paint her, to the beholder's surprise, she would be sweating inside this winter landscape painting. Sybil decided to first paint the parking lot. She picked up another brush and dipped it in the ocean-blue paint to design the Rolls-Royce. Off to the side of the park scene, Sybil would paint a piano with a bright light inside, highlighting a secret that would take hundreds of years to find out. The border of the whole painting would be a window frame that opened to show the whole scene. The window where the girls snuck out by the side of the newer section of Saint Francis made the day possible. The day itself made the painting possible.

During the spring art festival open house, the third-place winner would be a painting of celebrity Rob Lowe, completed by the girl who claimed he was her cousin. The second place would be a painting of the head of Pompey Magnus served to Julius Cesar, with a pompous fourteen-year-old Ptolemy looking on from the throne. The first place would go to a senior for a painting with a German title, *Unfug an einem Wintertag.* There would be two unexpected visitors to the open house. Drake and Wolfgang would walk around with the same smug grins that would be familiar to Sybil and Shay. They would stand in a crowd where the girls would see them, as Mother Superior would be announcing the winners. Wolfgang would smile after reading the title and say, "Mischief on a Winter Day."

Echoing throughout Cincinnati's East Walnut Hills area would be Sybil's voice singing as she played the piano. Her painting would be displayed and viewed by those who were impressed with the lines, shades, colors, and focal points. The cryptic window, so easily opened, awaited any girl who could hear the voice of its eerie silence, inviting an escape for the day. The painting and the window would silently mock the Saint Francis girls and the mobsters who court them.

# YAG

## San Francisco, California 1994

A group of thirty people, ages nineteen to forty-six, walk almost single file, whistling *Colonel Bogey March*. Some play it like a wind instrument on a thick, dried piece of grass they picked as they began the walk. They are approaching Yosemite Falls carrying light backpacks with water. They will stop to take a group picture. It's unseasonably cold for May, and they wear winter coats. This photo will hang in a frame in the church next to a space that awaits next year's photo.

The Church of St. Cecilia sat in the Cow Hollow area of San Francisco. It had been there, with its high ornate gables, since 1913. The local Catholics drove the expectations in the choir, the programs, and the school. In 1994, everything seemed to change for one segment of the church body. The largest and most popular group for young adults is now called YAG. Sitting in front of Leslie, in tiny elementary school chairs in a Catholic school cafeteria, were the other forty young adult professionals looking for the same thing she was looking for in the big city.

Leslie held a water bottle and sipped from it as she stood facing the other forty people.

"So basically, I went on what was supposed to be a three-day ski trip in Tahoe. I had put in for the time off legitimately. Well, fate had something else in mind. I broke my leg skiing down a challenging run, moguls and all. I was in the hospital in bad shape. This happened at the end of the trip, and I was in so much pain and so immersed in my situation that I never called work to tell them what happened. When I finally limped back in on crutches, they congratulated me on my two-week ski trip, and security showed me the door. People sarcastically applauded me out the door. I was done. That's why I'm here."

"Oh man, that sucks! I mean, we're glad you're here, that part doesn't suck at all, but your boss sounds..." Mike shook his head, and others nodded. They refrained from cursing in this church cafeteria.

Manny and a few others stood up to perform a skit to announce the next Yosemite trip. They exaggerated their quest as they pretended to hike up Half Dome and then sang a Beatles song about getting by with friends helping friends. They all shared shoulder hugs, and then one of them began doing leg kicks, which was unrehearsed, and Manny joined in, which caused laughter since it didn't fit the skit.

It was not uncommon for YAG members to sing or perform a skit to showcase the next dinner in town, service to the needy, such as fresh fruit sorting and dropping off for food deserts in the city, and other volunteer opportunities.

"So y'all come one and come all. We all have a load of fun together! Don't be shy now!" Like most others, Manny was from outside of California and had a southern accent since he had moved from Alabama and was not actually Catholic but Southern Baptist.

Tonight was a night when newcomers were welcome to share their stories, if they chose to. Leslie was led to share her ski accident that led her to join the group. Everyone clapped loudly and hooted. She took a little bow, and everyone made the effort to know her better. As Leslie started to work the room to reciprocate the welcomes, she felt a slap on her rear end. She jumped and for a moment thought she had made a mistake attending such a group, but as she turned around, she saw Tracy, a lady she knew from her apartment building. They both laughed.

"Isn't this an awesome way to meet new people? There's a lot of cute single men too!" Tracy said, and with a wink eyed the room.

The week before this, Darin's sister, Melissa, had moved to the Bay Area from Southern California. Darin, Melissa, and their other four younger sisters had grown up in St. Louis, Missouri, where the rest of the family still was.

"Okay, everyone, Melissa, folks!" Everyone clapped. Father Rogers smiled and asked what brought her to the Bay Area besides her brother, Darin. Melissa laughed at herself as though she knew her story would invite chuckles. Darin remained serious, his love for his sister trumping his ability to laugh at the incident he was about to hear.

"I was working for one of the big clothing brands down in LA, and gosh, it was thriving. I was so over the moon. I'm telling you it was my dream job. On top of all that, I fell in love with a man who I thought was a great guy. He was tall, handsome, funny, and his career was going so well."

"There's nothing wrong with that! The guy sounds awesome." Jenny screamed out happily, with the intent of supporting and welcoming Melissa.

"Oh, just wait!" Melissa cautioned her with a finger in the air, as Darin grinned at the group. Mike flipped his brows as if the story was getting good.

"We did our thing and got found out. Not only were we not allowed to be together since we worked together, but I found out the worst news!" Melissa continued, speaking with confidence to the room full of Catholic singles who sat in small chairs designed for elementary schoolers. For some reason, this made the room look more trustworthy.

"Oh my God, did you get pregnant?" Darin, her brother, mocked the question since they had heard it before. He and Melissa both shook their heads no, answering the question for everyone.

"I found out he was *married* to a lady who worked at the sister company, literally across the lawn from our building. I was temporarily transferred to San Diego while they conducted their investigation. I mean, it could have been worse, right? But when they completed the investigation, I was given goodbye papers. So I'm here. New job and Darin is my apartment mate." Everyone clapped.

"Gee, downfall is what brings people here?" Someone shouted out.

"The brokenness of the world has a way of driving the need for companionship. I've seen this over and over in my thirty years here." Father Rogers added, smiling as he looked around the room. Father Rogers kept a smile on his face when the YAG group met.

Melissa and Darin went on to share that they had four younger sisters who wanted to visit.

Nick leaned over and whispered to Darin, "Fix me up with one of your young sisters."

"Um, sure if you like them at thirteen," Darin said with a tone that showed he dismissed Nick, who now combed his hair at the break when everyone got up to go to the bathroom.

"Nick, you need to help me. My stepmother is evil, and I want to sue my whole family for everything they have. She blames me for everything!" Sarah had walked up to Nick after she and Jenny had discussed her situation. Nick continued combing his hair and didn't look away from the mirror.

"Well, if you want to come to the financial district and retain me, that's fine. Our firm charges a cool five hundred to over a thousand an hour. Your choice." Nick continued fixing his hair and checking his teeth as he spoke. Jenny and Sarah rolled their eyes. Jenny was one of the former models in the group, and any new man joining the group would turn to look at her, involuntarily. Other men who had been in the group for a while would say, "Yeah, she's really pretty. She is!" She seemed unaware of how pretty she actually was and had a constant smile on her face, always seeming to want to please others. Leslie and Tracy looked at each other and said,

"That girl has no idea she's beautiful!" After the break, David had a few announcements.

"There will be a *Wine and Cheese Wednesday*. Come one and come all." The women smiled when they saw the announcer, of Greek descent who spoke with a slight accent, and in his forties, like Nick. He had a successful business, and like Nick, he actually owned property in San Francisco. Both were no longer considered "young adults" but enjoyed meeting much younger women.

"What's your name?" Some of the new women shouted out. David covered his shirt with his hand, realizing he had forgotten to put on his nametag.

"Since I'm older than King David and have a Greek name that many can't pronounce, just call me David." The smile never left his face. The women smiled at each other, noticing how handsome David was.

Spinning through the crowd were the two ballerinas for the San Francisco Ballet Company. The YAG was for those roughly twenty-one to thirty-nine. David and Nick were on the older end, while the ballerinas were nineteen, so they violated the younger end of the church's definition of what a "young adult" is.

Nick and David immediately went up to talk to both ballerinas. Nick ran his hand over his hair before approaching them. David remained smiling and focused on the girls.

Women closer to their age waited in hope of chatting with David and Nick. Darin could be heard saying again how much he loves his sisters, but growing up, all he wanted was a big brother. People laughed and told him that maybe someday Melissa would give him a brother-in-law.

"Everyone, remember that we are doing the yearly excursion to the South Fork American River. Pack your wet suit, bathing suits, and overnight bags! It promises to be fun, and we can make s'mores by the fire at night." Patrick smiled, showing his crooked teeth after making his announcement with a lisp that he seemed to have had his whole life. He was tall and held a volleyball.

"Don't forget volleyball every Tuesday night. Don't be afraid. I know I look like I've seen a big volleyball before!"

Nick and David whispered while Patrick lisped through his announcement.

"Okay, last year on the white water rafting trip, there was Cheryl. She had…." As Nick spoke, David laughed because he knew what he was about to say. They said it at the same time, "Pubic hair hanging out of her bikini bottoms! More than I've ever seen in my life. Never have I seen a girl who cared less how she looked on the water." Nick laughed.

"She was hot and in shape, but man, I never expected the bonus bush. Did you know that when I was a kid, I found malted milk balls in the drawer by my parents' bed? Then, for the rest of my childhood, I was checking that drawer for malted milk balls. I associated that exact nightstand and any nightstand by my parents' bed with malted milk balls." David looked at Nick, confused about his malted milk balls story. "And…so?"

"So every year when we have the whitewater rafting excursion on South Fork, I expect there to be a girl paddling in my raft with mountains of pubic hairs falling out of her bikini bottoms." As Nick explained, David laughed and nodded, realizing that he felt the same way. Nick took out his small leather grooming kit, unzipped it, and began cleaning under his fingernails.

"God can't see what you're doing when it's foggy out, just like the t-shirt says. I think people on the raft trip always remember this." He and David then stared at the ballerinas across the room for a moment.

The YAG group was not above handing out private invitations for smaller parties, attended by only those invited and kept clandestine to honor the exclusivity. Nick and his brother owned a Dutch Colonial in Cow Hollow that had been in their family for generations. Everyone knew it was worth millions and the perfect place for a party. He handed out his invitations at the end of one of the weekly YAG meetings. Pretty Jenny, of course, was invited, as were the two ballerinas and David. Nick carefully selected who would be invited. He was careful, on the direction of Father Rogers, not to allow others to see the invitations flowing so as to spare hurt feelings.

"Nicky, I'm bringing my roommate Abby to your party," Jenny announced in a forward way. Nick smiled, knowing that only Jenny could get away with calling him *Nicky* and demanding to bring an extra guest to his party. Jenny was twenty-four but already too old for Nick and David, despite their being over forty. But Jenny never wanted attention from either of them, and this made her hard to read and someone more sought after. Most women in the group craved attention from these wealthy, handsome, older men. Jenny didn't care either way.

The night of the party meant a bouncer at the door, and folks on the guest list were the only ones let in. Jenny rolled her eyes after they said Abby was not on the list and pushed Abby to the main area, where there was a view of Alcatraz, the Golden Gate Bridge, and Angel Island. Nick grinned at Jenny and took both of her hands, swung them out by her sides, and spun her around, loudly saying,

"Now this is the formal attire that I would expect from my guests!" Jenny wore a very formal, long, black and white evening gown. Her beauty, combined with her classy tastes in formal attire made it all look easy.

"This is Abby, my roommate," Jenny said, smiling to the side as she introduced Abby and stepped out of the way, feeling she needed to after they had an incident at her Halloween party where Nick dressed as a rocker and scared Abby. To come up with a Halloween costume, Nick had reached as far as he could to be the opposite of what his daily life was.

"He's one of the top attorneys in San Francisco. It's a costume." Jenny reassured Abby after their Halloween party, as they cleaned up the next morning.

"He is frightening and gives me nightmares! I hope I never see him again!" Abby said, putting paper plates in a garbage bag.

"Oh, I'm dragging you to his formal party at his posh family-owned Cow Hollow Dutch Colonial. It has panoramic views and single men, darling, you're coming!" Jenny spoke playfully, knowing Abby would appreciate meeting new people.

As Abby stood before Nick, smiling, he looked at her carefully, and then took her arm, and without asking, began dancing with her. Abby was twenty-three. Jenny stood to the side talking with Darin and Melissa, who remarked that twenty-three-year-old Abby would be too old for Nick, who was turning forty-five. Abby allowed Nick to lead as they danced, and then at one point, rested her head on his shoulder.

"My God, Abby looks sixteen with those braces on her teeth! Are you sure she's twenty-three? Although looking sixteen is the magic formula for Nick, I think." Tracy, who had been in the group a while, shared her observations with Jenny as they got sushi and drinks from the kitchen buffet that Nick and his brother had put out.

"Yeah, the braces do make her look young. Her mom often calls our apartment to tell her she has to babysit their neighbors' kids in Orinda, where she grew up. That doesn't help either." They both laughed. Somewhere inside of Jenny was relief that Nick might meet someone and stop chasing her and leave the teenage ballerinas alone. Both ballerinas spoke to Manny, and as he tried to get them to dance, he could be heard remarking in his southern twang, "She twirls like that for a living! I thought only the Dallas Cowboys Cheerleaders had the right moves!"

Nick's brother tapped a wine glass with a spoon and, with a grin, put his finger over his lips. Everyone looked around to see what was happening. Nick then grabbed a microphone that they had plugged in near the dining room table and sang The Doors *Break on Through*. He was off-key, but everyone clapped at the end, saying, "Okay, he exposed himself!" Father Rogers made a brief appearance, had some ginger ale, and wished everyone well. Nick made him a plate, and Darin, Melissa, and others visited with him while he ate. Darin, noting the closeness of Nick and his brother, shared again with those listening that although he loves his sisters, he had always prayed for a big brother. People reacted with the usual "good luck with that," since they knew his parents were older and they had many children, similar to the other Catholic families. Father then left early while the party was still in swing.

"He's a well-fed man!" Said Manny, with every hint of wanting to keep seeing Father Rogers and the church supported.

The following week during the weekly YAG meeting, everyone sat in their usual small elementary-size chairs in the church school cafeteria, but in silence. People who showed up late looked unsure of what was happening and nervously looked around the room. It was an eerie silence. Father Roger stood up and spoke, unlike his usual self. This time, he sounded more like a major league football coach talking to a team that was losing the Super Bowl.

"What happened out there folks? What on earth? This is not who we are at all. This is an embarrassment. We have an obligation." Father's face turned red, showing a gin blossom as he patted his big belly. Everyone still sat quietly. Slowly, there were a few giggles. Jenny finally spoke.

"Well, as I see it, the kid is okay, right? I mean, he made it home and everything?" She spoke with a slight grin and a bit of sass in her voice.

"What happened?" Tracy whispered to Melissa and Leslie, who also slightly grinned.

"During the yearly zoo trip, where we take St. Cecilia kids to the zoo, we actually lost a kid. He was found in an area with wild animals where he was not supposed to be. Some kids are just spoiled. Personally, I think we should take kids whose parents would find a zoo ticket too expensive." Whispered Melissa, who, because of her brother Darin, knew the gossip of the YAG group.

After planning for better supervision for the following year's zoo trip, Patrick stood up with his lisp and mentioned the nursing home volunteer opportunity.

"Gladis has been more talkative, and I know that Harriet loves the attention. There's only one man left alive, and it's Herbie, who's 93." Patrick enjoyed referring to the elderly at the nursing home by name and updating everyone on their welfare.

Besides Darin and Melissa, there were assortments of siblings from large Catholic families. Tom and his twin brother Dometri, and their two sisters, who were also twins, did magic tricks. Tom, who was shy, performed most of them. They had grown up in the Bay Area in a place called Pleasanton. All four of them were regularly heard inviting YAG members to Pleasanton, stating what a lovely place it was. Strangely, no one in YAG had been out to Pleasanton and joked that it was an alternate universe. The girls shared that Tom had always been shy, so his parents bought him a magic kit when they were little, hoping to get him talking. It worked, they said. Tom embraced Magic tricks so much that during one meeting, he sawed Father Rogers in half as he lay giggling in the box. Everyone exclaimed, and even Father, still smiling, would not tell anyone what happened.

"Okay, folks, now we know what people do for fun in Pleasanton!" Leslie shouted out.

Abby skipped the meeting because she was too upset about the inconsistent communication with Nick. He took her out a couple of times a week and then would not call her. Jenny walked straight up to Nick, but stopped for a moment. He sat in the tiny chairs that the YAG members usually sat in, cleaned his fingernails with his high-end grooming kit, and was dressed in his usual designer shirts and pants that he wore to his law firm. This time, however, he had a sensitive, almost sad look to his face.

"Nicky, what the hell? Abby hasn't even heard from you. She was so upset that she stayed home tonight to hide." Jenny was still the only one who could call him *Nicky*. No one else called him that or ever had.

He barely looked at her. He looked beaten down. Jenny crossed her arms and tilted her head to the side.

"I don't know what in the hell is going on with you, Nicky!" Jenny gave up and walked away. Before the meeting adjourned, there was one more small group discussion about fellowship with others and how it enhances and supports faith. People were asked to share in their small groups examples of times when they felt close to others and how it increased their faith. This led to sharing how they also felt marginalized at times. To everyone's surprise, Nick shared that his family had moved during his junior year of high school.

"No one at our new school was looking for new friends. I'll say that much!" Nick tried to laugh, but it became obvious that this was linked with his not allowing others to get close. At the end, as people were putting chairs up as they often did to help Father Rogers out, Jenny shot over to Nick and said, "High school weirdness or no high school weirdness, you're calling Abby tonight. I mean *tonight*!" Nick grinned at her, still looking a little condescending, as if it was a privilege he had given her to speak to him.

St. Cecilia had a light on at night in the cafeteria once a week to accommodate the Young Adult Group, known as YAG. But every other week, there was another light on. This light was upstairs, above the chapel, in an out-of-the-way room. This is where MAG, also called the Mature Adult Group, met. Anyone over forty qualified for MAG. Tony, who was only thirty-eight, had met forty-six-year-old Peggy there. Both groups saw each other at volunteer opportunities such as helping at the nursing home or sorting fresh fruit to take to the food deserts of the city.

Every Saturday morning, those from MAG or YAG arrived at the church parking lot and began sorting fresh fruit into boxes that would have a variety that could be donated to those who needed it. This meant a lot of lifting and bending down. Tony and Peggy had begun a conversation, and despite her having joined MAG and Tony having been active in YAG, being that he's under forty, they exchanged phone numbers. Tony had lifted all the heavy boxes for Peggy, who regularly thanked him for his strength. This made Tony feel every bit a man. On the evenings when YAG met in the bottom level and MAG happened to be meeting on the top level, all Tony could think about was Peggy. During a debate about whether donating money to the homeless was a good investment and how it might be spent, he got up to get a drink of water. He could hear Father Rogers giving the final commentary, stating that helping those in need, no questions asked, was what Jesus would do. Tony's heart pounded, and he found himself drifting out of the back part, walking up the sidewalk, and into the front part of the church in the dark night, and climbing the carpeted stairs slowly, anticipating. He could hear the voices in the MAG group, having a similar debate, *using resources to endow others, and what would Jesus do today in San Francisco.* He saw the light under the door. The light grew sharper as it slowly opened and then closed again. Tony stopped on the stairs as he was halfway up and looked. He froze, unsure why the door opened and closed up there. He heard someone stumbling down toward him. It was Peggy. They began kissing on the back stairs of the church. Peggy would not allow Tony inside her North Beach apartment, so after a date, they would shake hands and he would give her a peck on the cheek. But at this moment, they needed no words.

As 1994 came to a close, Father Rogers conducted a *Marriage and Family Life* course required of anyone who wanted to marry at St. Cecilia. There were several YAG members and a few MAG members. Tony and Peggy, Nick and Abby, Jenny and a man named Jesper, whom she met at a party, David and one of the ballerinas with whom he got pregnant, Patrick, with his lisp, met a nice girl named Naomi, who was a master of the *Book of Ruth* from the Scripture. Melissa met a man in MAG on the one time she attended the Fresh Fruit program. His name was Art. He was quite a bit older than Melissa, but became a favorite of her brother, Darin, for the way he took care of her and helped her heal from her shame at having had an affair with a married man.

Darin himself was not yet enrolled in the course to prepare for marriage. He met someone special at the end of 1994 during a YAG meeting. When people were sharing stories during the group, someone had shouted out that Darin was finally getting a big brother, since Melissa was getting married.

"No, as much as I'm down for having Art as a brother, it gets better than even that. I need to share that during Thanksgiving, there was a knock on my parents' door. Of all people, I answered it thinking it was my aunt and uncle we were expecting. My mom was stressing over the turkey, and my sisters were all helping her. My dad was watching the game and basically yelling at the TV. I answer it, and there's a guy about a few years older than me staring at me. He says my dad's name, and I'm getting a strange feeling. My dad quickly turns the TV off and sits quietly. *Let him in…* he tells me and I do. I'm wondering what's going on, but I know this moment is holy. My dad stands up slowly, and the mystery guy and my dad stare at each other. This is my brother, who was born years before I was born and before my parents met. I talked to him and by the end of the night we talked and hugged and I knew I finally had a big brother!"

Everyone applauded, and Father Rogers smiled widely. For the whole year, and from the time anyone had met Darin, he spoke of wanting a big brother.

"Your story gave me chills! That is a beautiful story of God's love and what faith can do! My name is Elena." The new girl walked up to Darin as if she were meeting a celebrity.

"Welcome to YAG, Elena. I'm so glad you liked my story." Darin smiled at Elena. The other men grinned across the room, knowing this was a time for them to stay scarce. In good time, Darin would proudly introduce his "big brother, the one I prayed for my whole life" to the group. His name was Benny, and it helped that his big brother was single and handsome.

Tom and the two sets of twins would do another magic trick at one of the last YAG meetings that those getting married would attend. This time, his siblings stood up in costumes to help him.

"Today, we're going to make someone disappear. Any volunteers?" Darin's brother, Benny, stood up. Everyone exclaimed at once, even Father Rogers.

"No! We waited too long to find this guy!" Nick finally volunteered. Jenny turned her face to the side and smirked, knowing there were many times she wanted Nick to disappear. Her roommate, Abby, now sat proudly, wearing her engagement ring from Nick.

A large group of people approaches Yosemite Falls, whistling *Colonel Bogey's March*. Darin and his sister, Melissa, will bring a special guest named Benny. They don't know it yet, but they are safer this year with Benny. The blank space that awaits a photo in the church will show seven heroes who rescue a dozen St. Cecilia YAG campers who are left behind in the falls as it gets dark. Benny will lead the rescue mission with a few others, including Darin. He whistles just a little louder than everyone else, and the meaning behind it is far more compelling.

# You Don't Have to be a Star
## Atlanta, Georgia 1978

Rally could feel the wind in his hair as he skated quickly down the pavement, surrounded by red maple, southern magnolias, and flowering Dogwood trees on all sides. The sound of Marilyn McCoo and Billy Davis Jr. singing *You Don't Have to Be a Star* played in the background. He closed his eyes just a little to feel the music and remember 1978. To him, the song itself was about all the many loves, such as Eros, Philia, Storge, and Agape. Every kind of love he would long to have was all covered by the songwriters, James Dean and John Glover, in that one song. The sound itself made Rally feel more loving toward everyone around him.

Back then, the song's focus on love and what's important did not, however, curb his desire for fame. Rally skated hard around the corners, with music in his ears, and thought about his name in lights, commentaries talking about his performances, and guards escorting him through crowds in a hotel lobby. The desire was genuine then, and it was genuine now.

The house sat on Peachtree Battle Lane in Atlanta, Georgia, and was surrounded by homes of similar character, except that across the street stood a large mansion. This home was much older and was said to have been owned by various famous Georgians. Beverly lived next door and fancied Rally. But he said that although she was the most lovely southern belle, he didn't date tall redheads. This did not stop Beverly from coming over for dinner and showing her most caring side.

"She has designs on you!" His mama would look at him and firmly state this every time Beverly's name came up. Mama was not one to ever make an ill remark about others. She enjoyed Beverly but couldn't resist stating what she saw.

Thanksgiving meant the beautiful fall leaves were in bloom. The Sourwood, Dogwood, Redbud, and Sassafras were alive during this time. Anything could happen during the fall in Atlanta in 1978, and *the house awaited anyone who wanted to know its secrets*. When Rally first looked at the house, his mama excitedly urged him to make an offer on the two-story older home, with its ornate charm, hardwood floors, and crown molding and wainscotting. There were mature trees surrounding the home, and it sat lower than the houses across the street. The steep driveway was the setting of neighborhood kids' roller skating accidents, which led them to find Beverly next door to fix cuts and remind them that there was no broken kneecap. She spoke in a nurturing way in her feminine southern drawl, "No more tears, dear, no more tears!"

This house would be the perfect setting for memories in 1978. *It sat ready.*

Rally enjoyed the view from his office at the *Atlanta Star,* where his desk displayed pictures of his mama, his nine-year-old daughter Stacy, and ten-year-old son Jason, who were from two different ladies, and the recent birthday balloons and cards from coworkers celebrating his 32nd birthday. His mama, Henrietta, had no money and so could not live on her own. Rally never thought twice about having her move in because she was the center of his life and got on well with anyone he had over. As he finished the sandwich Henrietta had packed him, his phone rang and he quickly shot the wrapper into the nearby wastebasket, wiped his hands, and answered it.

"Rally, you need to come interview the young kids in the neighborhood. The early teens are starting a camp for kids. It's just precious. They have a schedule for them, matching t-shirts, and rewards. They are helping out parents who have to work in the summer. They hike through here every blessed day, and it's just so nice to see." Rally heard his mama's southern voice sharing what she thought was an ideal scoop for the *Atlanta Star*.

"Okay, mama. It sounds like a nice story. I'll need to get over there." Rally would agree with his mama whether he thought it was a good story or not. He was hoping to be granted access to some of the criminals at the local prison, some of whom were affiliated with the mob. He had been contacted years ago about an incident in New Jersey that he titled *Phony Cannelloni from Castalonni*. He was the first to cover it and received residuals when it circulated. He never knew how Tony Castalonni found him, other than that he said he asked around. This jump-started Rally's career. He had gone to the local prison in New Jersey so Tony Castalonni, who was serving life for multiple execution-style murders, could tell his story. Rally's calm, southern, and gentle nature was able to draw a lot of details out of Mr. Castalonni.

"Mighty nice to make your acquaintance. I'm Ralph Sherman, but you can call me Rally." Rally began with a handshake, treating Mr. Castalonni as a friend. He was invited to call him Tony, and that he did. Tony looked at him as though they needed no introduction or as if Rally had given him a fake name, almost rolling his eyes. It was as though they knew each other, but Rally didn't think they did.

"Tony, how did this work for so many years?" Rally asked, having turned on his tape recorder.

"We had the cooks wrap the cocaine or cash in plastic and put it inside some of the cannelloni and meatballs for certain customers. We would put extra sauce in a dollop pattern to mark the special meatballs or special cannelloni. The waiter, one of us, would serve the dolloped items to those who were expecting it. Sometimes they would get up, pretending to be agitated, and say they wanted more mozzarella on top and head to the kitchen. Police were casing the area and would show up as undercover patrons. This was the perfect time to box everything up in the back kitchen. We could attract everyone to one place and not be discovered. Police didn't check the area right before or right after the family got together. So if we boxed everything up in the kitchen by the time the family gathering was over, we could safely put the boxes away or put some into trucks. There was enough unmarked food getting served to undercover police, and we had our system. But we could wrap up drugs, money, notes, anything inside a meatball or a cannelloni. An informant served an undercover cop, and you know the rest. I'm sure you also read about the rival gang's involvement and the meatball murder?"

"So this led to what was called the 'meatball murder'?" Rally tried to act lighthearted as he asked Tony more questions. Tony went on about what the court already knew and what led to his lifetime conviction. Rally had asked unique questions in order to get more odd details about what happened. He wanted his story to go beyond just what was published in the court records. He was able to get odd details, some of which he wished he had never heard, but he knew would make for interesting and publishable details. Some were humorous, if murder ever can be. Tony shared that they thought one guy was dead, but his fingers were moving. There were multiple people buried alive. Some were tortured or promised release upon giving up names or addresses, but they were still tortured and killed anyway. One guy was still chewing his cannellonii after they thought he was dead. This part of the story got people talking and made Rally's story visible, along with his name. None of the violent stories surprised Rally, based on what he knew about the mob.

"How did y'all get my name?" Rally was amused as he asked this. Tony looked tough as he stared hard at Rally for a moment, the way a big brother stares at a younger brother.

"Let's just say I know a lot. If you need anything, kid, I'm here." Tony looked smart as he put out his cigarette in the little dish, as they finished in the dark, cement, designated interviewing room at the prison. Rally could see a distinctive frog tattoo on his arm. This made Rally laugh a little, simply because he was unclear what Tony could do for him from lock-up. It made the impression that mobsters continuously find themselves invincible. Rally still shook his head, laughing a bit as he exited the prison.

Every Sunday, he and his mama sat in church together, but it didn't stop Rally from craving a name for himself. The quest to be a humble southern man was encouraged, and although Rally had all of that on the outside, inside, he wanted fame so badly that he almost had to remind himself to breathe. He sat in church and thought about his children, Jason and Stacy. He taught them to be humble. He would ask them how a troubled classmate at their school was doing and ask how they had helped them.

But today, on this warm, green, and floral summer day, a far cry from the dank prison, he stood interviewing kids in his own yard.

"Well, now, how did y'all decide to start a summer camp for the wee ones?" Rally smiled as he asked questions of the teens who started the camp. His mama looked on, smiling, since the story was right in their backyard.

"Mr. Hopper across the street, you know, in the big mansion, he's covering the cold drinks and ice, and some of the materials for arts and crafts. The little kids seem to like it, and it gives the parents a break." The two 15-year- olds with braces spoke excitedly. They were cousins, Jimmy and Cindy, and they posed together for a picture in their camp shirts.

"Well, now, what's the name of your camp?" Rally asked, forcing himself to be of good cheer but dreaming just a little about a more compelling story.

"It's the Peanuts Gang!" The two teens spoke in unison. "Well, now y'all have just made my day! What a wonderful thing to do for the youngsters!" Rally smiled as he finished the interview. It felt as if the house had pulled Rally closer on that day.

"Mama, do you know when Mr. Hopper is home?" Rally figured she would know this, since she was home all day. Mama looked confused for a moment and then hesitated as she looked around the street.

"The mansion, Mama, Mr. Hopper lives across the street." Mama nodded as if she was unclear what to say.

"I believe you could go over whenever you see fit." Mama sipped her cold, sweet tea that she had brought outside as she looked down. Rally walked quickly up the hill with his camera and recorder and knocked on the door. Mr. Hopper did not answer at first. As Rally turned to walk away, the door opened. Rally stood smiling with his camera, microphone, and recorder.

"Mighty fine to meet you, sir. My name is Rally and I live across the street." Rally smiled but could see in the man's face a familiarity that he couldn't understand. The man smiled as if he knew who he was. Rally looked at him a little bit sideways, still smiling, and then Mr. Hopper mirrored him by looking at Rally a little bit sideways, still smiling. Before he could ask any questions, Mr. Hopper answered them.

"I am happy to help the Peanuts Gang. Mothers and fathers work hard for a living, and they need a place for kids to go. Some of the arts and crafts are a good idea, you know, so they can get out of the hot sun." Rally found himself speechless and did not know why.

He went skating again at his favorite park. He turned a sharp corner, listening to his music and again asking himself what love really is. Every day, he asked himself how many forms of love he had seen that day. He thought of the Eros, Philia, Storge, and Agape. Seeing the kids talk excitedly about the camp and learning how Mr. Hopper helped without being asked, and how Mama had noticed, felt like a day's worth of love for Rally. He had enjoyed meeting Mr. Hopper.

"Yes, who is this? Really? How soon?" Rally tossed his wax sandwich cover in the wastebasket and stood up, grabbed his tape recorder and briefcase, and set off. As he drove to a coffee cafe to interview another self-proclaimed mafia affiliate, he could hear the latest song on the radio, A Taste of Honey's *Boogie Oogie Oogie*. Rally wondered again what his mama's love meant and if he would find his daddy. Being the age he was, it was still important for him to find out who carried love in their hearts, and what kind of love they embraced. He had investigated who his father might be when he wasn't investigating the mandated stories for the *Atlanta Star*. He knew that his neighbor, Beverly, seemed wired for all four kinds of love. His quest to know who carried the four loves was not a thirst he could quench easily. It went with him to every interview.

"Hey, sit down!" The nervous, Italian, bald-headed mobster affiliate signaled for Rally to be seated. He looked from side to side, and his hands shook as he raised his coffee mug to take a sip. Rally smiled slightly and looked at him a little bit sideways.

"So what brings me here?" He asked the nervous man, who continued looking down, sipping his coffee.

"Someone is being made, but he has to get rid of our problem first. I want to warn you so you pass it along."

Rally still stared at him sideways the way one looks at a thirteen-year-old trying to act older than he is. The man was in his fifties, and Rally knew that. He also knew that every time someone's life was threatened, they would come to him. He was the *Atlanta Star* contact person for the mob. This had happened by accident when he was young and new and had interviewed one of the uncles of the man who now sat in front of him. This made him the contact, even more than a decade later. He knew when they were afraid for their lives and would come to him.

"So tell me more. I'm not sure I have a story yet." Rally spoke fast for one born and raised in Atlanta.

Thanksgiving brought rain and floods. Before the rain, Jason and Stacy, Rally's kids, had arrived from two different places, dropped off by two different mothers.

"You done good with this house, Rally," Henrietta spoke calmly as she sipped tea right before the kids arrived.

Henrietta made apple fritters and Jambalaya to prepare for all the excitement. The house smelled of both, and the kids brought an energy to the new house that any newly purchased old home would await. They ran through the house, played board games, and told funny stories to Rally and Henrietta.

The rain continued falling and filled the front yard. Across the street, the homes were set up higher, and the water made its way down to Rally's yard. Mr. Hopper came down, out of breath, shook his hand, and wished him a happy Thanksgiving. There was something about him that made Rally feel he needed to know him better.

"You need to get Henrietta and the kids out of here. The rain will fill up your living room and the whole downstairs." Mr.

Hopper's southern accent sounded different from his mama's accent and his own.

"My house is on the floodplain?" Rally looked helpless as he asked this.

"I was hoping it wasn't." Mr. Hopper nodded at Henrietta as she appeared standing behind Rally. He could see the two of them making eye contact. This response was confusing to Rally.

Sure enough, Rally's kids came running out of the house, laughing and screaming. The water began flooding the downstairs. Rally parked his car at the top of the hill and went back inside as the rain poured down and thunder and lightning crashed. He began carrying everything he could upstairs. The power was now out, and he had to carry everything up in the dark.

"Can I help you?" He heard a deep voice with an unusual southern accent. It was Mr. Hopper again.

"Yes, Sir, I would welcome it. Much obliged." Rally's southern hospitality never left him, even when roles were unexpected. Mr. Hopper had the kids and Henrietta stay across the street in his large home on the hill that was not in any danger of flooding. While he and Rally carried the furniture upstairs piece by piece in the dark as the thunder and lightning raged and the water poured into the living room, causing the water level to rise three feet.

Rally thought again about the many loves and considered it as Mr. Hopper, who was about the same age as his mother, tirelessly continued to help move all couches, tables, beds, and anything else from the first floor, upstairs. He noticed how they were the same height and build and made the same noises as they carried heavy items.

The next story Rally was asked to cover was the *Minks*, a story about a large group of ladies in Atlanta who have weekly lunches around town. The group had grown larger by the month, and since many of them wore designer items and reserved tables in the most expensive restaurants, they were called the Minks. As the group grew larger, people in town would gossip about when and where they spotted the *Minks*. It now became a newsworthy story.

"Well, now how did y'all get started?" Rally asked, smiling kindly.

"We need to fix him up with Geraldine! Look at that, Shelby. He's handsome, young, and carries himself like a charming gentleman." The ladies smiled as Shelby, the mother of Geraldine, stared warmly, with a hint of lust. The ladies sipped their sweet tea as the biscuits were brought to the table, and all laughed at the idea of handsome young Rally, journalist from the *Atlanta Star*. Then one lady, Olga, got serious and began sharing about the history of the Minks.

"We have been lunching together for over a decade, and we are now noticed by the rest. Don't you know everyone wants to be part of the Minks now? We won't be able to make a reservation big enough. We want to welcome all the ladies, but tell us how!" They all laughed as Rally's photographer took photos. After speaking with Olga, he pulled the senior coordinator, Shelby Buchannan, well-known in the Minks, aside so he could get her story separately. She invited him to call her by her first name, but Rally addressed her in the old-fashioned Southern way by putting Ms. in front of her first name. Ms. Shelby shared that they began this ritual when they all graduated from high school in 1945, got married, and are still together today in 1978. The papers were starting to print: *I saw the Minks today*. It was more appealing than spotting the Oscar Meyer Wienermobile. Rally printed what they ordered for lunch, who paid, how they chose the restaurant, and how establishments attempted to lure the Minks for publicity.

"We have a standard, which is five-star restaurants. Nothing below that is part of our plan." The coordinator shared, with no hint of arrogance but rather a *matter of fact* sharing of how they do things in the Minks.

"Well, that's just mighty fine. Y'all deserve the top of the heap. Tell me this, when do your daughters become old enough to join the Minks?" Rally had no air of judgement, but instead sounded connected to their happiness. Inside, he did wish for some type of fame or fortune that would allow him just a little more of what would make life easier for Mama, his kids, and himself. As he started to finish the interview, he remembered to ask himself how many loves he had seen that day. This prompted another question that he began asking as his feet were pointing the other way toward the door.

"Do y'all ever want to donate to any causes? I've heard y'all are very philanthropic." Rally had made the last part up, hoping they would rise to it. The coordinator of the Minks smiled at Rally calmly and nodded.

"I'm glad you asked that. We have a hotline where people who need help can call in, and we decide as a group which one we want to donate to. Sometimes, individual ladies will donate to an extra cause on their own. It doesn't matter how we help people or who helps as long as they get help." Rally's face turned red as he smiled widely. This lady, who appeared to live well and was carefree and opinionated, had just unassumingly disclosed all that they did to make life easier for others. She would not have stated it if she were not asked. This made it more pleasing to Rally. When he published his story, he titled it: *Minks Not What You Think* and thought about Agape love.

The flood raged on, and those like Rally, Mama, and his kids, Jason and Stacy, stayed at a hotel despite Mama saying many times that Mr. Hopper had invited them to stay at his mansion. Since he was going back and forth to the house and the kids, he decided it would be a good idea. Those like Mr. Hopper and the Minks were not on the floodplain, so they had time to socialize. Mama had been so excited about their buying the house on Peachtree Battle Lane that Rally just couldn't say no. He never checked to see if it was on the floodplain.

As the rain subsided and the water damage was repaired, they all moved back into the house. Rally listed the home for sale with the new knowledge that this flooding would be a yearly occurrence. For a time after the flood, no one asked to walk through the house. At dinner one night, Rally said to Henrietta, "Mama, I'm asking Geraldine to dinner. The Minks coordinator, Ms. Shelby Buchannan, is fixing me up."

"Well, now she sounds just delightful. I hope y'all have a wonderful time." Mama lifted her tea glass and winked. But Rally didn't get around to asking her out. Shelby had told much about Geraldine on the phone.

"She's 28 and has never kissed a boy. She wants her first kiss to be from her husband. She's a very special girl. She needs a southern gentleman like you." This type of love was appealing to Rally, but it almost felt too big for him. He kept it in a box in his heart, safe, where he couldn't fail. He thought about her, based on the picture he had seen. She had high cheekbones, nice skin, light brown shiny hair, and stood a little shorter than Rally. The added bonus was that Shelby had shared that Geraldine enjoyed roller skating at the same park where Rally skated.

The next holiday visit from Jason and Stacy meant a trip to the movie theater to see a movie that had more killings and blood than expected. Stacy snuck into Henrietta's room, too scared to sleep in her own bed, and Jason snuck into Rally's room for the same reason. Henrietta had an early morning doctor appointment, and Mr. Hopper across the street was kind enough to drive her while Rally went to work. That left the kids home alone.

"Hello…yes, okay. Well, that sounds mighty nice!" Rally hung up and called home, waking up Stacy.

"Now y'all need to make all the beds, wake up Jason, and let the Realtor and prospective buyers in for a look-around. We're still trying to sell this house."

"Yes, sir!" Stacy answered and did as Rally said. However, Jason did not get up. When the realtor headed upstairs with the young couple, they enjoyed the size of Rally's main bedroom, but then asked what the door in the corner went to.

"It's the attic, Ma'am." Stacy shared, hoping they wouldn't open the door. Sure enough, the realtor and young couple opened the door to the attic, shone a flashlight, and looked around, remarking about how big it was and how it could be an expansion of the main bedroom. Then they jumped in surprise and exclaimed. There was laughter. Stacy turned around, embarrassed. Jason, who wore his white underpants in the classic briefs style and nothing else, hid with his hair sticking up, standing in the corner of the attic. The realtor had shone her flashlight around to show the young couple the vast space and flexibility it gave them. None of them had expected to find a young boy hiding in the attic in his underpants.

"Oh, no, does he come with the place?" They laughed and remarked.

"No, Sir!" Jason answered in a humble air.

Stacy explained that it was her brother who didn't quite wake up fast enough to get dressed.

"Have y'all ever had a flood here?" The couple asked Stacy, and she looked at the realtor. There was a long silence.

"The realtor will oblige y'all." Stacy was not going to lie, not since Rally and Henrietta had taught her not to. But she didn't want to be the one to describe the flood of 1978.

That day, Henrietta was gone most of the day after her appointment. Rally went across the street and knocked on Mr. Hopper's door to ask where she was since she had been taken to a doctor's appointment by him. To his surprise, she looked frazzled, waved him in, and then, before he could realize anything, paramedics arrived. Rally looked around while the paramedics attempted to revive Mr. Hopper. Rally wanted to give space to Mr. Hopper, so he had gone into one of his large rooms. There was the library, the garden room, the office, and a large dining room. Rally stopped in surprise, and his feet couldn't move. He saw his very own baby picture and pictures of his mama when she was young, posed with Mr. Hopper, who was also young in the picture. There were pictures of Stacy and Jason as babies and more pictures of Rally. Rally quickly made his way into the foyer, where the paramedics attempted to revive Mr. Hopper. He felt he was floating as his feet took him from room to room for no apparent reason. He felt the Storge and Agape love that took no effort. He made his way back to where the paramedics were and could see a frog tattoo that matched Tony Castalonni's. Henrietta began providing documents to the paramedics and was heard saying, "Ralph Antonio Sherman Castalonni from New Jersey." Rally was breathing hard. He could not review in his mind the many loves. He had too many thoughts.

"Mama…mama?" He spoke, but Henrietta was not able to answer. He stared helplessly at Mama and Mr. Hopper. Rally walked in a circle and didn't take his eyes off his mama. She was the center of all that he was, and now he experienced a shift in who he thought he was. It was as if he were spinning as his feet whirled around the new reality of who he was, *who everyone was.* Beverly had agreed to walk to Rally's home and watch Jason and Stacy, who were still there. This gave him time for everything to sink in and settle.

A week later, Rally sat across from Tony Castalonni, who smiled widely.

"When were you going to tell me? Froggy Sherman Castalonni is my daddy." Tony smiled and, for the first time, didn't look so tough. He looked clean, vulnerable, and as if he had awaited this moment.

Henrietta had wept in front of Rally and the kids.

"He wanted to be something big for you. He wanted to leave a legacy. But he had to save his life." Was all she could say.

The house on Peachtree Battle sat there for a reason. It had awaited the insistence of Henrietta, who insisted that Rally buy it, and the suggestion from Mr. Hopper. Henrietta would not live anywhere but Atlanta since she was a tenth-generation born and raised Georgian. Henrietta had wanted them in close proximity to Rally's daddy, even if he didn't know who he was. The flood had provided them a chance together to save Rally's belongings that made the house a home.

Rally skated hard around the corners, through the trees on either side, and thought about the many loves. He still needed to remember all that had happened and how he would write it for the *Atlanta Star.* Would the title be *Froggy in Witness Protection?* He turned the corner hard as he thought about his favorite song that seemed to drip about the four loves, *You Don't Have to Be a Star* by Marilyn McCoo and Billy Davis Jr. played in his head again. He turned and found himself bolting into the grass, hard, dripping with sweat. He had wanted to dodge hitting someone since he was going too fast. *Someone* had done the same. Rally sat up and met her eyes.

"Much obliged. My name is Rally." He got up and shook her hand. She smiled, having also been skating too fast.

"Charmed and delighted, Rally. It's Geraldine."

Rally smiled.

"You can call me Gerri." Geraldine was everything that Ms. Shelby had said she would be.

"Miss Gerri, would you come say howdy to my mama?" Geraldine smiled widely. This moment was written on everyone's hearts and definitely existed somewhere on Peachtree Battle Lane.

Would he be able to understand this many loves? If the Peachtree Battle Lane home could plan, then it had everything to do with this moment. They both stood staring at each other, feeling the weight of the whole world, past and present, in that one moment. Rally felt like a celebrity. But the weight was light, just for Rally and just for a moment.

# The Celestial Hotel

## 1994

Large pictures hang in various parts of the *Celestial Hotel,* almost telling the history in a timeline. They go back to 1889. The first employees saw the invention of cars, and a common coachman became a chauffeur during his long tenure at the *Celestial.* Some employees had a lifetime career in their position with the *Celestial Hotel.* Sean had passed the pictures on the wall many times and carefully perused them along with his coworkers. They had laughs over what people in their positions would have looked like in days before. The uniforms and hairstyles had changed. But there was something everyone seemed to overlook.

At the top of a hill with a city view at night and enough trees to keep Doctor Shirley happy sits *The Celestial Hotel.* She and her husband, Theo, had stayed here many times before, especially when they wanted to get some of the five-star cuisine. This time, Shirley traveled alone to complete her sabbatical, which would be an anatomy book for undergraduates. Theo was a travel writer who would be sending the mystery guest to evaluate the entire operation of *The Celestial Hotel.*

The doorman, Sean, had been there almost as long as she and Theo remembered. He regularly greeted her with a smile and by name.

"Shirley, my girl, how's Theo? Y'all got a new dog this year? That other one is as old as Abraham Lincoln. How are the kids? Out of the house now? Girl, you look good as always. Traveling alone, huh? Well, they got scallops on the menu and I know you're going to like that! Make your reservation for the private conference rooms because they'll fill up quickly. Oh, and don't worry about the ghosts that they talk about here. They don't hurt anybody. Although I don't think you ever did worry about it."

Sean, known amongst all the hotel guests as the cordial gentleman who enjoyed nonstop talking, seemed to remember names, faces, and situations. Shirley disliked talking, and that was her original attraction to Theo, who, similar to Sean, spoke nonstop whether anyone was listening or not. This trait endeared Shirley to both personalities. Sean spoke differently to men and could be heard saying to another male employee, "Man, your sister's just never gotten her freak on. She needs to have a good time, man."

Next, Shirley was led over to the front desk, where she met Susan, who checked her into her room.

Susan had worked in the basement as a hotel operator, and when she began dating a limo driver, Lawrence, who served all the hotels in the area, she applied to work at the front desk.

"So I have been meeting Lawrence every night that I'm here, assuming Fawn's not working." Susan smiled deviously as she and Patricia ate in the basement employee cafe, *Parasols*.

"I thought your mom only worked the same nights as you, so you don't have to pay separately for parking." Patricia pointed this out and took a bite of her meal, eyeing Susan and laughing. The *Parasol Employee Cafe* had food from the five-star hotel restaurant *Celestial's Finest Chophouse* brought in daily, allowing employees to eat the previous day's leftover five-star menu.

"Fawn can't know I'm seeing Lawrence. I told her I'm looking into a second job to pay for my own car." Fawn was Susan's mother, who worked at the hotel's kiosk.

"Did you know about me and Jeremy?" Patricia shot her eyebrows up. Susan smiled at the idea as Patricia began explaining why she and Jeremy were meant to be.

"He knows I was placed here for him, and if he doesn't know that, then he's rebelling against the universe," Patricia spoke with angry passion in her voice. Jeremy worked at the concierge booth which was right near the kiosk.

After lunch, Patricia excused herself as Susan went back to the switchboard to answer phones. She wandered up the back staircase to see who Jeremy was talking to. She could see Fawn selling gum, candy, and mints to various guests from the Kiosk. Jeremy was busy telling a guest where to catch the ferry and places to grab lunch across the bay. Patricia smiled to herself.

"Hi, how's it going?" Patricia greeted Fawn, who was surprised to see her, and then leaned into the window and whispered. Fawn looked shocked and angry. Patricia then turned around to see if Jeremy was free yet. Zelda eyed Patricia, so she quickly went back down the back staircase and into the switchboard room, where Susan continued answering calls cheerfully. Sometimes Zelda would call upon Patricia to interpret at the front desk in Malay, her home language from her birthplace of Malaysia.

When Susan's shift was over and Erika came in, Patricia smiled and said goodbye to Susan for the night. Before Susan walked through the dark accounting area, the three girls reminded each other that they were going out for Erika's birthday next week. When the switchboard calls died down, Patricia, with a big grin, spun her chair toward Erika.

"Did you hear? Susan is seeing Lawrence, the limo guy. They had an encounter in the back of his limo. Fawn said she can date anyone but not a married guy." Patricia laughed as Erika looked puzzled.

"How on earth would her mom, Fawn, have found out?" Erika asked, and then the switchboard rang, and they both took calls.

The *Parasol's* employee cafe also provided bread, tuna fish, peanut butter and jelly, fruit, cereal, and other items that some of the younger employees and single parents brought home. Sharon had walked in late at night when only the night watchman was in and spoke partially to herself and partially to him.

"I'm a single mom, and I really thought little Jarod and I were going to be homeless last year. Now I'm saving as much money as I can. They don't ration what we eat in *Parasols,* so I'm stocking up. I never want to be that scared again." The night watchman, sipping coffee and eating one of the famous *Celestial's Finest Chophouse* danishes, winked at Sharon in understanding as she took out her Tupperware, opened the lids, and put tuna fish, fruit salad, hot rice, chicken and vegetables in the Tupperware and screwed the lids on tightly. She then took several of the small individual boxes of cereal and also put a whole loaf of bread in her backpack. There were many loaves of bread, and they were known to go bad if the employees didn't eat them fast enough.

"I was raised by a single mom too. You'll be all right. Your boy will always love you. Good for you for looking out for him." The nightwatchman grinned warmly. Sharon nodded in exhaustion and smiled a bit. While the drama with Patricia, Susan, and Erika went on, she only wanted to get her son Jarod to a stable place.

"How's it going in the operator room? Do you like it?" The nightwatchman then asked. Sharon smiled thoughtfully.

"Yes, I'm earning eleven dollars and twenty-nine cents an hour, and that's more than I've ever made. We have a nice two-bedroom, two-bathroom house with a little yard. It was Anthony in Reservations and his partner, Travis, who found it for us. When they had an overstock of mattresses, we were able to get nice beds. There's even a room for my mom because Travis walled off an extra open area that may have been an extra living room. I'm happy." Sharon smiled gently. The nightwatchman looked as though he were an angel and would have created that for her. But as he sat sipping his coffee and eating his danish and Sharon continued loading her backpack with food, they were quiet. When their breaks were over, they would return to their places in separate parts of the hotel.

The next day in the *Parasol Employee Cafe*, as Susan and Patricia sat eating on their usual break, Zelda came in, having come all the way downstairs from the front desk. She was clearly angry and spoke in her German accent.

"Why was there a big verbal altercation between Fawn and that limo guy, what's his name? It was embarrassing! Fawn says that you told her that Susan was dating him. We all know, as do some of the guests and folks about town, that he's married and just had his first child." Zelda stood panting, out of breath, having walked all the way down to the basement from the front desk, and filled with adrenaline. This caused Susan to stare at Patricia angrily. Patricia looked helpless.

Shortly after this, Susan put in for a transfer to the front desk to avoid Patricia and be seen more closely by her mother, Fawn. Likewise, Zelda could allow Susan to help interpret in Bahasa Indonesian, Indonesia being where Fawn and Susan were born.

Susan could see Jeremy at the concierge desk talking to guests. When he needed an Indonesian interpreter and waved her over, she sauntered over, knowing full well what her conversation would be after they were finished helping the guests. Susan stood at the concierge desk, explaining to the guests in Indonesian where the museums were located, how to board the ferry, the ins and outs of the trolley car routes, and some recommended lunch spots. When they thanked her and moved away from the counter, she smiled at Jeremy. This was her moment.

"So Patricia is so in love with you. When will you make your move? I mean, she's obsessed. Come on, give the girl a break. You're all she talks about day and night. She believes GOD put you two together, and you're disobeying the universe if the wedding isn't being planned soon. I figured I would give you the word so that maybe Patricia might have a conversation about someone or something other than you." Susan grinned, knowing by the look of horror on Jeremy's face what she had just done.

Bradley called a meeting of all the operators, and it was to be held in the boardroom at the upper corporate level of the hotel. He came running into the boardroom the way a motivational speaker with a large following does. The girls hooted and cheered for him as he shook his rear end and went around sitting in different ladies' laps as they affectionately said with a song in their voices, "Fatima…Fatima!" Erika was the only one *not hooting, not calling him Fatima, and not allowing* him to shake his rear while sitting in her lap. Sharon, who greatly needed her job to take care of Jarod and her mom, Lil, who was almost seventy, and the rest of them, went along with it. Bradley announced that Susan had transferred to the front desk. Patricia announced that they would celebrate Erika's birthday at the Embarcadero. She invited everyone, but knew that it would only be herself, with Susan and Erika. This was assuming that Susan had forgiven her for telling Fawn she was seeing Lawrence.

"Why are we calling Bradley Fatima? I'm Catholic, so I can't do that. He's not the mother of God, he's not Madonna." Erika spoke in a forward way, causing Bradley to eye her angrily.

At the end of the meeting, Lil could be heard saying, "Amen!". Bradley quickly corrected her, saying, "No, it's gay men! We will end every meeting that way." Most of the ladies laughed, some forced a laugh.

Back at the switchboard, this would still be a topic and would cause Bradley to retaliate.

"Why aren't you calling him Fatima, like the rest of us?" Patricia asked. Erika spun her chair around and stared hard at them as if they were ignorant. Her disgust was evident.

"I'm Catholic, and Fatima means mother of God. Besides, his name is Bradley, last I checked." Bradley kept a mean, devious grin on his face and reminded her to make the guests' welcome cards using the letter blocks and then update the menu for the *Celestial's Finest Chophouse*. A few reservationists from the next room could be seen looking without being obvious.

At the boardroom in the early morning, before too many guests awoke with requests, there was a meeting of the Front Desk, concierge, and kiosk. Jeremy was celebrated for his tenth year at The *Celestial Hotel*. Everyone clapped, and he received a pin and a symbolic key that allowed him two free nights at the hotel, which was what was provided for those with tenure of a decade or more.

"Anyone special you'd like to bring?" Zelda asked with a teasing grin.

"Actually, yes. There is someone I'll be inviting." Jeremy's face turned red as Susan stared at him.

"Well, we need to book you pretty soon, so give the dates to Reservations." Zelda encouraged. Susan agreed, mostly wanting to know if it was Patricia.

The switchboard, being next to the Reservations area, allowed Erika to check for arrival dates and names. Susan and Patricia had not spoken since she became aware of her having told Fawn about her involvement with Lawrence. Erika saw the date of Jeremy's check-in coming up and asked Patricia if she had any special plans or fun dates coming up. She wanted to know if Patricia would be his special guest.

"No, I just cook and watch movies. I will make chicken and potatoes, and then sometimes take myself to the movies. I saw Aladdin recently." Patricia spoke in a mundane way. Erika waited until she went to the bathroom and then took the wake-up call lists and requested a 6 am wake-up call for Jeremy and whoever he stayed with, so they would be rudely awakened during what was supposed to be a romantic stay. She made sure this would be done when Lil was working. She didn't want to threaten Sharon's job since she was so frightened for herself and her son, Jarod. Lil, being older and having worked for the *Celestial* longer than anyone, was in no danger of losing her job.

"I need to show you something because you're going to find out anyway." Erika showed Patricia that Jeremy had plans to spend two nights with a lady in the hotel, to celebrate his decade of employment. This caused Patricia to talk angrily during their whole shift, in between answering the switchboard.

"God gave him the chance to be with me, and he denied the very directive of the universe that told him that we are to be together! This is dark behavior that will only lead him to the very destruction that I tried to get him to avoid... he is turning his back on the design for his life... he knows we are destined to be together..." Erika nodded as she made the guest welcome card with the letter blocks, as Bradley had told her she needed to do, since she refused to call him Fatima. Patricia continued her rant during their entire shift and even as she exited the switchboard room to leave the basement.

When Patricia started to exit to the outside city noise and landscape, Sean, the doorman, already knew about Patricia's heartbreak. Susan, who now worked at the front desk, couldn't help but smile since she wanted Patricia to feel a little wrath for having told her mother about her married lover, Lawrence.

"Girl, I'm so sorry you're hurt. You know what? There's always more fish in the sea, you know? Even if Jeremy is not the right guy for you, there are so many others just waiting. Don't sit around waiting on a man who doesn't regard you. Do you know what I'm saying? There's always something better around the corner, so don't despair. Just keep hoping. I mean, don't you want someone who thinks you're just the finest thing?" Sean went on even after Patricia had walked away, talking to herself. Sean spoke about the situation, as Patricia also said to herself as she walked away. The two continued simultaneously, conversing with each other in different parts of the city.

Sure enough, Lil called and woke up Jeremy and his girlfriend in the very early morning, causing him to complain to Zelda, who knew nothing about how it got on the wake-up call list. Lil was not in trouble because the request was simply put in the pile with no employee name stating who took the request before her shift started. Employees of *The Celestial Hotel* could always blame the rumored ghosts.

During her next shift, Bonnie from Reservations poked her head in and said, "Patricia Lah, how was your weekend?"

"Bonnie Lah, it was good? Please tell Erika Lah that she needs to call Bradley Lah Fatima, and let him sit in her lap, or he's going to keep dumping extra work on her, Lah!" Patricia spoke cheerfully, trying to help Erika.

"And what's the thing with putting Lah at the end of everyone's name?" Erika asked while making even more welcome cards for guests.

Shirley sat in the private conference room with a cup of tea from the *Celestial's Finest Chophouse* and a plate of fruit. She began writing about the importance of food to each organ in human anatomy.

She did a chapter on each organ, what it contributes, and how they cannot work separately.

Jana came over to chat with Anthony, who was the senior reservationist. Jana had been in the accounting office for a while and knew numbers well, but had a troubled marriage and was rumored to be spending private time with Reggie, an executive from the sales corporate offices upstairs.

"They took my car away from me, so I'm bumming a ride from Joann in Housekeeping. I don't know when I'll get it back."

"Jana *Lah Lah*, that's not nice! You need your car! At least you didn't have to worry about parking today." Patricia laughed.

"How many Lahs do you know to put after someone's name? Did you put two *Lahs* in because of Jana's sad story?" Erika asked, her tone embarrassed them a little since she really wanted to know about the game and how this came about.

Patricia wore a cheerful face, and this made Erika proud. During the break, Susan came down to speak to Patricia.

"We're taking you to dinner and then to Embarcadero for your birthday. Does that sound okay?" Susan and Patricia stood together smiling. Erika was impressed that Susan had forgiven Patricia and that Patricia could at least pretend to move past her obsession with Jeremy.

In the *Parasol Cafe* sat Sharon before her shift, eating soup and a plate of an entree she got from the hot and cold bars that was the five-star menu from the previous day, which included Chinese chicken salad and Tasmanian salmon. The nightwatchman also came in since it was right before his shift. He filled a plate and sat with Sharon. Sean came in singing and saw them both.

"Now that lovely lady Sharon, who is sitting right there, well, I have a story about her! I was walking around during my break, and I saw the nightwatchman, and we started walking around together because we're getting claustrophobic here, you know. Well, what do we see but the saddest lady in the world sitting on a bench crying. We started talking to her, and she said she's about to lose her apartment, where she takes care of her mama and her little boy. What do we do but we take her over to the back of the loading dock of the hotel. Every time they fire someone in this hotel, the Human Resource Director, Josianne, sends her assistant out for a latte and tells her to stay gone for a while. When this happens, everyone knows a position is opening up."

Sean continued as he loaded his plate with saffron risotto, East Lothian beef, and chicken tagine. Sharon smiled as did the nightwatchman. She interrupted Sean to share her side.

"Okay, this is where I got a little creeped out. I didn't know who you people were and why you were telling me to go with them. I didn't know if you were going to kidnap me or what. When you said a job at a hotel, I was concerned you were trying to sell me into a life of prostitution because they said a hotel, but you were not walking me into the front lobby, you were walking me into the loading dock, and then into a back area that's all cement. Luckily, I saw the *Celestial* Human Resources sign and Josianne. I was still not sure until I actually started working here and saw my first paycheck." Sharon laughed, and the nightwatchman smiled gently. As they all ate, Sean talked nonstop about how he would never hurt anyone and how his mama and daddy raised him right.

No one had seen Bradley at the *Celestial* for a while. Erika was no longer assigned any guest welcome cards, didn't have to hear about not calling him Fatima, and their meetings were run by either Anthony or Zelda, and neither of them demanded a chant of "Gay men!" at the end of the meeting.

During the Embarcadero birthday celebration for Erika, there was a musing about where Bradley might be. Patricia and Susan didn't seem worried or interested.

"But he's your Fatima, remember? Aren't you worried about him?" Erika asked with a slight smile. Susan and Patricia grinned and were more focused on eating their ice cream as they all looked out at the water from a bench.

"So, are we okay without Jeremy? Are we okay without Lawrence? Where is the healing process, ladies?" Erika asked as she also ate her ice cream.

"Hey, it's nothing this thing can't fix!" Susan picked up a joke gift that they had given Erika. It was a Magic Wand that came with directions.

"Oh, it's the ultimate gift certificate! Come on!" Patricia said with excitement. They held it in their hands carefully after they were done with their ice cream. Erika demonstrated, reading the instructions. When she reached the part about "Speak clearly, and don't be embarrassed." For some reason, this made all three girls laugh.

Would they wish for mind control over Jeremy or for Susan to be allowed to date Lawrence? Would they wish for nice things for Sharon and her son Jarod? Erika secretly had a bad feeling about Bradley and wanted him to be well. Erika had joined in putting Lah at the end of people's names. Patricia had been nicknamed Miss P.

"Miss P Lah Lah, my wish for you is that you find someone better than Jeremy. More magical and just for you. Miss Susan Lah Lah, my wish for you is to be liberated from living at home and also find love with a single guy. I wish Sharon would win the lottery." Erika waved the magic wand for each request, and they all three gave their approval.

Sharon would wait the following week outside the Human Resources office with the ambition to interview for a reservationist job that could lead to a corporate sales job after. She had to wait extra long since Josianne had sent her assistant out to "get a latte and stay gone for thirty minutes," so Sharon knew a position was opening up. The cook had been giving orders to the other kitchen staff, going against what the head chef had said. This resulted in a physical fight in the kitchen. When the cook was put on leave, he concocted a story about slipping on a soggy corn flake and injuring his neck. They were overstaffed in the kitchen anyway, but needed more reservationists.

As Erika entered the hospital room to see Bradley, the nightwatchman was leaving and smiled at her. Bradley seemed connected to him with his eyes. Erika sat at the bedside and observed that Bradley looked very weak. He would die a few days later. His partner, Johnathan, was there, weeping in the corner. Erika was unsure if Bradley knew who she was. She had hoped he would have the same connection as with the nightwatchman.

When she reported for her shift, she asked the switchboard operators and reservationists if they planned to see Bradley. They shrugged it off and continued bantering back and forth, putting Lah at the end of everyone's name.

Doctor Shirley could be heard lecturing in a large conference room. Her charts were placed on the projector to illustrate the harmony of human anatomy. She had spent her time eating in *Celestial's Finest Chophouse* and lounging in various parts of the hotel, where she would sometimes see Sean.

"My arthritis is acting up, and I'm eating less sugar because of my diabetes. I exercise every day and eat my greens. Did I tell you my left hand sometimes gets stuck, but I know if I twirl my wrists..." Sean would go on, and this would make Shirley smile.

When Theo finally arrived, Sean escorted him to where Shirley was staying. He had already published his findings based on what the mystery guest had experienced. He had many positives about *The Celestial Hotel* and even noted the generosity among employees toward one another. But his report noted verbal altercations between employees and loud conversations about relationships. Guests overheard some employees confusing them by addressing each other with *Lah* at the end of each other's names. One manager was even referred to as *Fatima*. The most written letters of compliment went to a man named Sean, who was the doorman who managed to remember the names of people's children, what they were in town for, what they did for a living, when they were last in town, and what their favorite foods were. The lights would go out unexpectedly in the lobby and many of the guest rooms.

Sean, Susan, Patricia, Sharon, Erika, and the nightwatchman on their breaks stopped and listened to Doctor Shirley's lecture on anatomy for a few minutes as Shirley lectured to a room full of undergraduate pre-medical students.

"The organs work in synchronicity to keep the body functioning. No, we are not as strong as our weakest part. We are better than that even, the compensatory mechanisms help the body as a whole function well. The interdependence of our organs allows the whole part to thrive." Shirley smiled. There was something that both Dr. Shirley and Theo's mystery guest missed. It was the large photo on the wall of *The Celestial Hotel* that showed employees from the time the hotel opened. No one seemed to notice that the nightwatchman had appeared in every photo for over a hundred years, looking exactly the same. Doctor Shirley could not explain this to her students. Even Sean had not noticed.

The lights went out for a moment and then came back on. Of course, Sean and the rest of the hotel staff always blamed the ghosts. Sean would talk nonstop about the spirits in the hotel and how they influence everything, while pacing the corridor where all the photos of the hotel hang.

# About the Author

Greer Sickinger-Maher is a long-time elementary school teacher. She earned her undergraduate degree in Creative Writing and a Master of Science in reading strategies, and always knew she would be a writer and educator. Greer Sickinger-Maher has been writing stories since she could hold a pen and telling stories since she could talk. She has resided in Texas, California, and Ohio. She is currently a public school teacher in Ohio and happily married with a grown son.

www.ingramcontent.com/pod-product-compliance
Lightning Source LLC
Chambersburg PA
CBHW070752180626
46818CB00007B/3089